SICK BONDS

A Novel By

SIMONA MIHUȚIU

Book translated into English by:

Ovidiu Constantin Cornilă

Paramount
Book Publishers

SICK BONDS

Out of the spin of fate, the immortal Furies, the vengeful goddesses of Darkness, with their spindles of yew wood, were twisting the past, present and future of mankind, tracing its destiny and punishing it for its crimes. Clotho was reeling, Lachesis was weaving, and Atropos, the 'one with no turning back,' as her name suggests, was cutting the thread of life. Maybe justice was being done, maybe they were just fulfilling the human inevitability, or maybe it was just hatred punished by other hatred...

Fortuna labilis and the theater of forbidden souls

The writer from Oradea, Simona Mihuțiu, surprises us again, skillfully and interestingly, with a more than original creation, allegorically titled *Sick Bonds*, a book printed in 2024 by Total Publishing, Bucharest.

As in the case of the play, *Hope Never Uses the Elevator* or of *Tales from Senior Help*, the writer from Bihor proves a sixth sense of writing, deep, subtle and refined.

Right from the novel's title page, the narrator warns her readers with an explanation of the three Furies, she says, "vengeful goddesses of Darkness," who apparently have the power to alter time, but not in any way.

Thus, the reader can somewhat imagine what is about to happen (a false appearance), although, at the end, he or she will feel disoriented, overwhelmed, and, as the undersigned himself declares (after two readings), identified with the main character.

In his or her passage on this earth, man has the opportunity to accumulate various experiences, some of which disappear and others, which remain impregnated in the being for three more lifetimes and an eternity. Some of these experiences are not forgotten for good, others for evil, and some of us become slaves to our own sins, this would be an attempt to define the volume of prose in question.

In extensor, and from the very beginning, I would like to mention that Simona possesses the excellent and very rare quality of playing: between the lines, between thoughts, with the characters, with feelings, with the narrative thread, and, above all, with time. What we have here is a book of destiny, of an existential drama that does not have much reason to envy the great classics such as Jane

Austen's *Pride and Prejudice*, Victor Hugo's *Les Miserables*, and then the Tolstoyan *War and Peace*, among many others.

Simona Mihuțiu appeals to an extremely complex and diverse register of inner turmoil, which she then leaves, as it were, in the hands of the three furies I mentioned, Clotho (clothes in English), Lachesis (poisonous snake) and Atropos (the one without a place). He cleverly resorts to symbolic names, speaks through them, assigns them at the opportune moment, which makes the distancing attitude in the flesh of the narrative apparent, not final.

At first glance, *A View to a Kill*, if I may use Ian Flemming's expression of Agent 007's address to *Sick Bonds*, would be a classic, with a typical plot. The reader discovers a family of modest origins, which has two daughters, Amalia (the beloved, from *amor*, *bitter*) and Malvina (which may come from *malvado*, meaning evil). As in any family, there are definitely favorites and least favorites. Who is the beneficiary of the attention? As always, the black sheep of the family. Well, this villain breaks the scheme of the natural, of logic and, aided as if by providence (or perhaps by the three Furies), deliberately destroys on various occasions. First, when she steals Dorian from Amalia, her sister (Dorian, a symbolic name clearly related to desire, desire, but it also becomes, at some point, Satan, in Amalia's vision, a kind of *daimon* (demon) or intangible Eminescu's dauphin or lighthouse), or when Lili, Amalia and Dorian's daughter, dies in a car accident when Malvina was driving it. Moreover, Malvina runs away with Dorian to America, and their union gives birth to Marlene, who resembles Lili (*ecce homo*!). Simona Mihuțiu introduces in the novel a detail-argument about the names Lili and Marlene: as a child, Amalia received a doll she called Lili-Marlene, whose head she had torn off so that she would not have to share it with her sister. No comment...

Throughout the plot, the main character is involved in a factual plethora that leaves the impression of interminable. We seem to have before our eyes a soldier with a thousand lives, treading on a minefield without caring that he is paying an exorbitant price. Right from the moment, he enters the game of death, the soldier engages in the maelstrom of the inevitable: explosions, thrown by them over other mines, rip him apart. The action becomes a never-ending game, a Rubik's Cube with no end in a labyrinth with no way out. Yet, in all this huge conflict of souls, caused by Amalia's stubbornness to forgive, her envy of Malvina's undeserved success in life and her continual going against the tide of fate, there is a compensation, skillfully introduced by the author in a confessional tone, on three occasions. The first, by Cornelia Aludean, her mother, who gives her a providential reply, one of the keys to the novel: "Forgive me, Amalia, if you can... forgive them all... that you may forgive yourself."

The second time, the same forgiveness is asked of her by her sister Malvina, who is on her deathbed: "Forgive me... she squeezed Amalia's hand." Finally, on the third occasion, Marlene, having arrived in Lugoj from America, when Amalia tells her that Malvina has died of Covid, confides in her aunt, saying that Lili, her half-sister, had told her: "Forgiveness brings healing and hope. I believe so."

Forgiveness is, therefore, a solution to annihilate envy. Through hope, one can forgive, through love, one can forget. Easy to say but hard to do, especially when destiny is put on automatic pilot to play tricks.

The few moments in which Amalia accepts reality are when she realizes the existential conglomerate of her own being, from which she cannot escape: as a pupil, she had been a docile nerd with no life experience, she had had a child with a man opposite her temperament, smart (on top of that, he is also an engineer. This does not necessarily mean that all engineers are nice people or smart, sic!), with a joke always in his pocket, but who, unfortunately, had run off with her sister, albeit a treacherous, more beautiful, adventurous and, above all, always favored by fate. She realizes that she is a sentimental misfit, a prisoner of a dismal past. She cannot overlook her mother's second-rate love and a sister who steals the man of her life (Dorian), who has two other husbands (whom Amalia is jealous of, displaying an obvious Rebecca complex), and who "always had what she wanted [...] and always got rid of what she wanted to get rid of." Trapped in a vortex of the past by transmitting the obsessive sensation of returning to the place of her birth, to the different reliving of a dream that could have been real, Amalia feels the heavy burden of her decisions or, as Nietzsche called it, *das schwerste Gewicht*, alluding to the myth of eternal return, an impossible one in the case of the character created by Simona Mihuțiu.

All of these events prevent her definitively and irrevocably from living her seventy-six years in the present, a time clearly situated at the confluence between understanding and death.

The inner voice of ambition and ego consumes Amalia synchronically. The obstinacy of her stubbornness to find solutions, to approach diplomatic ways when life demanded it, to accept the antagonism of external reality-inner voice, led her to create personal protection: "[...] Amalia had found her own weapon of self-defense- a wall between the world and herself."

Furthermore, another facet of Amalia's drama of refusing reconciliation and forgiveness occurs when, back home from America, in an episode of sisterly dialog, Malvina informs Amalia that Dorian had died years before of galloping pancreatic cancer. At that moment, Amalia feels a sense of relief as an effect of the desire for revenge that had been smouldering in her soul for so long. Here, dare I say it, our heroine herself becomes a vengeful goddess of the Darkness, as Simona Mihuțiu says in the explanatory motto-like paragraph on page 5. Maybe, somewhere, justice was being done, that human inevitability meets a dead end, or maybe it was hatred punished by other hatred.

When the soul burns, when life consumes you like perpetual combustion, the lack of forgiveness becomes a habit, and life lessons are never learned because life itself has been lived as it is written in the book, in the unfavorable sense. As Andrei Pleșu says: "If you are trained as a good student, you begin to believe that all the answers are in books." *Quod erat demonstrandum.*

Similarly, when the soul is hardened, the feelings become sharp, rigid, and the inner eye plays a theater of absurd tragedy, perhaps undeserved by anyone. Shortly before Malvina's death, Amalia sees her deformed sister, at a closer look, having one pupil larger than the other. Ignoring the dying woman's plea to forgive her, Amalia replies in her thoughts: "No, no, Malvina! Only God forgives. I am not God."

The truth accepted by Amalia is the truth that she secretly fabricates for herself, deliberately confusing the element of reality by superimposing it on the imaginary. Marlene thus becomes Lili, called without right of appeal in memory of her dead daughter. From this ludic of identities, the main character takes a giant step to reach the climax: at Marlene's (now Lili) request to visit Malvina's grave, Amalia takes with her a sprig of green-leaved yew, a plant that makes red, poisonous fruit (leitmotif) in the shape of a candle. Ex nihilo nihil fit.

In her essence as a contradictory character, through her modus vivendi, typical of the concept of singularity, as isolation, or oneness, she opposes duality, the pair, hence the source of all the evil that befalls her, that follows her and defines her destiny, beyond her relationship with the mythological Furies.

They say that every man has the unequivocal right to make choices. Between right and wrong, everyone can choose what makes him happy. Loosely translated: as you lie down, so you sleep.

Of course, what has been captured in these lines is merely a *captatio benevolentiae*, because the narrative fabric of the book, through its exquisite, carefully chosen lines, through its short, sometimes blurred sentences, through the whole set of details made available to the reader (where antagonistic ideas of the innocent-reluctant type abound, truth-miracle), make up a vast exposition of sensations very similar to Scheherazade's stories. This fact tempts the reader to postpone his sleep, arm himself with a large cup of coffee and let curiosity run free.

Through *Sick Bonds*, Simona Mihuțiu proves herself an excellent weaver of existential threads, a scenographer of mental movies, a redoubtable observer of dreams/visions called people, clinging to the capricious goddess Fortuna in snatches of time.

Ovidiu Constantin Cornilă
Madrid, 27 decembrie 2024

Chapter 1

The room gave off a shabby and heavy feeling. It lacked any attempt at interior design, any care to create a more hospitable space. But it would be too much to expect hospitality in an attorney's office. The peeling walls and metal cabinets reinforced the gloomy impression. It was the year 2020, but it could just as well have been any other year from the turn of the previous century, given the decaying air and the whiff of the stale that reigned in the room. Files were scattered everywhere, open or tied with string, some lying on the floor in disarray. The old clock above the entrance ticked dully, as if it, too, indicated that time was adrift in this space.

It was hard to tell whether this room infected attorney Dinu with its anguish or the man's personality had taken its mark on everything around. Most probably, both could be considered. In any case, the impression was one of perfect symbiosis between space and person.

The old woman sat seemingly quietly on the uncomfortable step in front of the desk, analyzing attorney Dinu's stern face. She had been there for a quarter of an hour, but besides the fact that the man had greeted her and formally invited her to take a seat, he didn't seem to notice her, flipping through a thick file.

"If he hadn't been so stubborn, he might have been a handsome man, she thought. So young – I don't think he could be more than fifty – and so devoid of the joy of life! It's no good! Not good at all!"

She looked toward the barred window, then back at the desk. "As if I were elusive," she said to herself. She noticed the sterilizer on the corner of the desk and the fact that the attorney wasn't wearing a mask. She would have taken hers off, too, feeling she was suffocating, but she didn't dare.

Eventually, the front door suddenly opened and a policeman

entered the room.

    – Aye, sir. The chief attorney has ordered us to take action in the "Disinfectants" case. He needs all of us. We'll leave for Buziaş in a few minutes. I came to let you know.

    – Very well. The attorney's displeased face contrasted with his words. The corner of his mouth twitched slightly in an intermittent rictus.

    – Allow me to leave! The policeman sketched a gesture of putting his hand to his cap.

    It was only after the policeman's exit that Dinu looked overtly and attentively at the old woman in front of him. He noticed a gentle look in her eyes, coming somehow from far away, from her old age. His face was quite wrinkled, betraying her 75 years. There was no trace of coquetry. Her white hair, still rich, cut short, was uncombed. Dinu wondered if the woman in front of him had been like this in her youth, if she had had the same simplicity. Without realizing it, he found himself sympathizing with her. She reminded him somewhat of his own grandmother, perhaps because of the gentleness she radiated.

    "It's a good thing I'm wasting my time with a bitter grandmother while others are busy doing serious things!" The old woman's presumption of innocence insinuated itself into the attorney without her even realizing it, just as she failed to realize that it was the first time this had ever happened to her. His profession had taken its mark on his personality and his way of relating to the people around him, especially those who had the misfortune to pass his office. He even had a saying of his own, of which he was very proud: "paranoia keeps you alive." He was aware of this professional flaw, but he told himself that there were other jobs that deformed human nature. Besides, his profession made him feel stronger, more in control, an undeniable advantage. He wouldn't have changed it for anything else, even if there were moments of dissatisfaction with the less spectacular files he was working on that had no chance of propelling him up the professional hierarchy. He figured that it was exactly such an insignificant file that this one would be opened in order to close it. Anyone can denounce anything, real or imagined.

He hated informers, but he was duty-bound to verify accusations to look for evidence, and he needed them. Is that what this was all about?

– Thank you for coming, Mrs. Amalia Aludean.

"As if you have a choice when you're called to the district attorney's office, what could I say?" – thought the old lady.

– You should know that our conversation will be recorded. You have the right to call a lawyer...

– Do I need a lawyer?

The woman's eyes suddenly widened. They didn't express fear, just blank wonder.

– Uh, not necessarily. But it's a procedure, we have to say that... You're not accused of anything.

"Yet," Dinu would have added, if anyone else had stood before him. The word, however, did not fit the elderly woman in front of him.

– I called you as a witness.

– Witness? Witness to what? The old woman seemed genuinely astonished.

– In a moment, let's not be hasty. You can take your mask off if you feel more comfortable without it.

– Ah, thank you! So hard to breathe with it! replied the old woman after making sure that the man in front of her was serious. She took off her medi-mask and put it in her pocket.

– Your name is Aludean Amalia...

– Yes, it is, she confirmed.

— What have you been doing, Mrs. Aludean?

— I'm retired, she informs him calmly.

— No, no. What was your profession? Unwittingly, his tone takes on a warmer tone, led by the old woman's voice.

— Assistant biologist.

— Where exactly did you work?

"What a habit they have of asking you what they already know! What a waste of time! He thinks I'm naive," Amalia thought to herself.

— At the hospital, in the lab for a while, then I worked at the Pohalma Fruit Farm. The salary was better...

— Oh, with Mr. Director Ştefănescu...

— I worked with him too. I worked mostly with Mr. Pora. Do you know him?

— No, I don't know him.

— I thought you knew him... in our town, almost everybody knows everybody. Lugoj - small it was, small it remains!

— But beautiful and full of history, Mrs. Aludean! I forgot to offer my condolences on the death of your sister...

— Thank you! said Mrs. Aludean with a sigh. What will you do to her? Malvina was five years younger than me... She could have lived. Oh! There's no way to know God's plans in advance... But... I always thought that I, being older, would be gone first... It's not how we plan.

— Was she usually a healthy person?

— Yes, as far as I know... It seemed so... She was pretty spry for her years. Unlike me, who suffers from ulcers and was recently diagnosed with heart disease... How do you think this bloody COVID could take her so quickly?

— You think she died of COVID-19?

— Well, why else, good God? I've lived a long time in this

world, but I've never known such a pandemic! And so many dead! God forbid and protect!

— You didn't have COVID?

— No. Or if I did, I don't know. They say on TV that there are mild forms or even without any sign of illness. In any case, nothing bothered me. But, Mr. Attorney, I wore a mask everywhere, even if it was hard to bear it! I've disinfected all the food packages, the clutches, even the entrance mat. I followed all the instructions. That's why you called me, isn't it? You think I didn't...

Dinu stared at the woman. Unintentionally, he took pity on her. As far as he had been informed, her sister had been her closest relative... He thought how sad it is to be alone, especially at such an old age, to have no one to rely on, no support...

— Were you married?

— Uh... No, she hesitates. Well, it wasn't meant to be. I got used to taking care of myself.

Dinu comprehended that he had been stirred by a memory full of sadness, sheltered in the mists of time.

— When did your sister come to the country?

— It's over two months, at the end of February. My darling! It's as if God wanted her to die at home, having lived so long among strangers. She told me she wanted to spend the last years of her life with me, that we'd been separated for so many years... You know, she left the country under the communists, many years ago, after high school. Around '68, I think. She left with a folk dance band for a contest in Belgium and never came back. And from Belgium, he went all the way to America! You can imagine what was in our hearts, mine and my parents, because they lived at that time and they were hard-working people. My father was a tanner and my mother a tailoress. But they worked hard so their daughters could have everything and go to school. Back then it was...

– I see. You must have been very glad to have her back, Dinu interrupted the old woman's flow of words.

Once again, he remembered his grandmother, who would start to talk to him about something and if she was left, she would ramble on until you couldn't remember what the topic of the conversation had been. That was until the time came when he couldn't remember much of anything, no events, no people. Still, old age is ugly! The woman in front of him was still bearing her years well, with dignity, but who knows what the future might hold for her?

Dinu thought it seemed strange to add the notion of the future to an elderly person.

– Why not? Amalia Aludean quickly replied. The woman's eyes carried the gentle glow of an inner light. At least, Dinu thought so.

– You have been with her during this period since the pandemic began...

– Yes, it was just the two of us. We didn't go and we didn't have any visitors since the restrictions started. We respected the Emergency Ordinance! Only Agatha, a relative of ours, came. And our neighbor, Mrs. Grosu, too, but that was before the number of cases started to rise in our house around the beginning of the pandemic. After that, she stopped coming, too. We only went out, you know, on the strictly necessary occasions. We obeyed everything they said on TV because, being both old, we were afraid of this damn virus. If they said old people should stay indoors, we did.

– So you're saying that you don't know your sister to have suffered from any illness. Am I correct?

– She was very active for a 70–year–old. She didn't show her age. I don't know if she had a more hidden illness, she never told me.

— What were your sister's symptoms?

— At night, she was fine. But in the morning, she said she felt sick, her stomach hurt, and she could barely stand. She was sick and vomiting. Then she figured maybe it was the food. But all he'd had was buttered toast and tea. That couldn't be it. She was very dizzy. I don't cook heavy food because I have a stomach ulcer. I don't salt much, either. Dr. Marge, you may know him, he diagnosed me with ulcers. Good doctor! It's too bad they closed his department. He didn't deserve it...

— And after that? What happened? He was sorry he had to interrupt her, but he couldn't let her keep on talking!

— Then she asked me to take her to the bathroom. She was like a rag, flagging. She rinsed her face with cold water and asked me to take her to bed, she wasn't feeling well. She began to breathe heavily, shivering. And her pulse was weak, as far as I could tell. That's when I freaked out and thought it was COVID, they've reported cases of this before with sudden onset symptoms. I'd gotten hold of one of those quick antibody-based tests, you know, to have in the house just in case. I tested his nasal secretion, and it came back positive. I informed them when I phoned the ambulance, but Malvina was already unconscious and with low blood pressure by the time they arrived.

— Was she unconscious? She couldn't speak? Dinu seemed puzzled, searching for something in his papers.

— Nonsense. She was saying something incoherent, mostly meaningless syllables... Oh, God... Poor thing! Amalia covered her face with her hands, shaking her head. I'll never be at peace because she came to this country and got this. Maybe if he'd stayed in America until the pandemic passed...

— Can you tell me who gave you the test?

Someone from the hospital got it for you?

– Yes, a former colleague's daughter. She works in the lab, but, you know, I wouldn't want her to get in trouble, because she's been so nice to me...

– We'll see about it.....

Dinu types something on the computer.

– I'm sorry, Mrs. Aludean, that I caused you so much distress by reminding you of this trouble. I am sorry for your loss!

– Thank you, Amalia whispered.

– They didn't do another quick test?

– You mean the emergency services? No, they didn't. There was no time to waste, really. They said she had a very slow heartbeat. I thought that's what they said. They gave her norepinephrine, if I remember correctly, and oxygen, and then they took her to the hospital, took her to the ICU, to the COVID, but she died there a couple hours later.

– Do you remember how long after you called, the ambulance arrived?

– I don't remember exactly. It seemed like forever to me, because Malvina was getting worse and worse, and I didn't know what to do. I was desperate!

Something of that desperation was still echoing in Amalia Aludean's words.

– I see...

– Do you have anything against the Emergency Service?

– No, no... They did what they could and what they did best. We're at war! Even in war, things are not normal... I know from my parents. I was born in '45, the war wasn't over yet..., and you know what it was like afterwards, the famine that followed... It wasn't easy for anyone. As a child, that's what I remember, we often ate only bread with marmalade... We were happy when we had that! I'm afraid those times will come back! God forbid! But I was upset because I couldn't say goodbye to Malvina. They put her in a black bag like a vermin and I was not allowed to go near her... Even the funeral wasn't what it should have been! I don't even want to remember! We're Christians.

— Did your sister come to visit? Dinu changed the subject.

— She told me she wanted to stay permanently, to unite our solitudes now in old age.

—'Yes, yes, you told me,' Dinu wrote in his notes. Interesting. He hadn't been in the country for a long time if I remember correctly.

— A quarter of a century. It goes like this.

— Any children?

— A daughter. Uh, Marlene. She lives in New York.

— I see.

"If you understand, enlighten me, because I didn't understand at all why she came," Amalia thought.

— The girl never came to the country for the funeral.

— I called her, but she didn't answer. I texted her...

— I see. One more question... Who made the burial decision?

— The hospital. They said they couldn't keep the body too long, that it's COVID and they have a lot of deaths and they don't have room... Since I was the closest relative here...

— I see. Okay, Mrs. Aludean, thank you for making the effort to come all this way. I'll draft the statement and ask you to kindly sign it at the end. After you read it, of course. Please write down the name of the person who gave you the test. If we have any further clarifications, we will ask you to come again...

— Yes, of course, she replied, trying to sound benevolent, but at the same time hoping never to have to enter that building again.

The clacking of keys drowned out the silence, just as Amalia's old heartbeat was so obvious that she was sure anyone could hear it...

The attorney held out the statement for her to read, but the woman excused herself, forgetting her glasses at home, unable to read, so Dinu read what he had written to her himself. Amalia signed and then left, relieved to be out of that oppressive room, although the echoes of fear persisted and her heart continued to beat wildly... She stepped with a small, measured pace, trying to contain the urge to make a run for it. She didn't think the surly attorney would bother to look at her from the window, but she was a believer in the proverb "better safe than sorry."

When the policeman returned to the attorney's office, he found Dinu at the window, watching Amalia Aludean as she walked away, walking slowly and a little awkwardly.

— Our trip has been canceled! announced the policeman, without being asked.

— How come? wondered Dinu.

— They must have 'leaked' the information that we were going to go over their heads and canceled the meeting.

— Oh! The interlopers roam free and I'm sitting here interrogating nice old ladies, said Dinu, moving away from the window. A nurse woke up to complain that Mrs. Malvina Prudel didn't have COVID, but she was declared "COVID death." PCR test at the hospital was negative. Only the rapid, nasal secretion, antibody-based test her sister did before the ambulance arrived was positive. Hmm... These rapid tests — I don't know, really, how much confidence to have in them! In any case, all sorts of nutters are filing stupid complaints and I'm wasting my time with bullshit and craps!

— Well, somebody has to deal with that too.

— If Malvina Prudel hadn't been an American citizen, I wouldn't even bother. Or maybe that's why I should leave it this way. You never know what these foreigners think. How the hell was she buried without her daughter's consent? Everything's all messed up since this virus!

— Yeah, yeah. Do I have anything else to do?

— Not today. Tomorrow, you'll call the mortopathologist, don't let anyone say we didn't take care of the case. Go on, I'm getting pissed off! This morning has flown by without doing anything important.

Chapter 2

There were still few people on the streets. The two-week extension of the Emergency Ordinance on pandemic restrictions had come to an end, restrictions that had almost paralyzed almost every activity in all areas. Still fearful, people preferred to stay in their apartments or houses, the luckier ones. As in the besieged fortresses of former times, the walls of the dwellings provided a sense of temporary security. But here, the besieger remained unseen.

It seemed that the sky itself had put on a mask of clouds, with a late autumnal look, far too gray and unusual for mid-May in the Banat! Amalia took a more remote route, along the banks of the Timiş River, eager for a walk and having no desire to hurry home. Nature was full of life, unconcerned by the occasional invasion of viruses, throwing reality into the background. Some acacia trees still held their clusters of white blossoms, freshening the air. Here and there, swathes of purple iris elegantly decorated the wider green spaces, and tastefully trimmed yew shrubs lined the riverbank on its both sides, showing the viewer their stubbornly resistant red flowers. To Amalia, they looked like little candles... She wondered how many people knew how toxic this plant could be. How little of its leaves, stem and flowers had to be ingested to poison someone! An infusion, a cup of tea could kill someone. She was aware! After all, she had gone to biology school, even if she didn't graduate. As beautiful as they are, so toxic! Isn't life like that? – Amalia pondered.

She crossed the Iron Bridge. A family of swans was gathering their chicks towards the shore. It wasn't the first time she had stopped to watch and admire them, impressed by the mother swan's care for the cygnets, but especially by the male's attention to the female, staying together for the rest of their lives. This was family! Birds could teach people how to live together. Watching them, she couldn't help but compare it to her own existence. She,

Amalia, had never had a real family! A few reckless chicks tried to stray away, only to be quickly brought back into the group by their parents with a warning flapping of wings. Once – how long it seemed to her since then – she used to walk by the river with Lili, her daughter. She liked swans, too, especially the young ones. What a cuddly child Lili was!

Another swan timidly approaches the group. She was the one left alone after the death of her mate and was trying to start another family. But she was pushed away aggressively. Amalia watched pityingly as she was forced to move away. That swan will die. It will end alone. Was there any difference between her fate and that of this swan? When time will come, not even its last song will be heard by anyone... She realized she was lonelier than she had been for a long time.

The thought crossed her mind that by dying, Malvina, her sister, had escaped the loneliness of old age. However, twisted in all sorts of ways, this thought was not meant to give her the inner peace she would have wished for.

Amalia imagined she should have felt at peace and... free after her sister's death, but she didn't. She had the eerie feeling that Malvina had gone "to the afterlife," but she left her shadow everywhere and a mocking snort of laughter that Amalia could hear as if it were as if it had been a dream, especially in the middle of the night, like those words that had managed to blast the truth in her face:

"It was me behind the wheel." The peace that she had hoped to find at last, as a state of inner peace, a reconciliation, a redress of wrongs, was late in Amalia's life, and she was convinced that it would never come again.

– Good afternoon, Mrs. Aludean! a familiar voice roused her from her thoughts.

The old woman turned away, unhappy that her thinking had been disturbed. However, she managed to greet Mrs. Grosu, her next-door neighbor, a full-bodied woman, about middle-aged and very nosy, as many acquaintances had described her. The neighbors were mourning the recent loss of her husband. Mrs. Aludean remarked that she was accompanied by a man, a bit short and ugly in Amalia's opinion. After all, they suited each other. Neither of them wore masks, which have become compulsory on the streets and in public places.

— Hello, neighbor. Out for a walk?

Amalia smiled broadly at Mrs. Grosu.

— I wouldn't have gone out, she replied, but I have to stock up. We have to...," she corrected herself.

Amalia noticed the widow's embarrassment.

— Uh..., introduce yourselves: Nelu, my boyfriend, Mrs. Aludean, the neighbor from apartment 8.

— How do you do! Nice to meet you, the man said kindly.

— How do you do! the old lady replied.

— Have you heard about Pantelimon on the third floor? They took him last night by ambulance to the hospital. He's in ICU in a serious condition. They say it's COVID, but I don't believe it. That's a figment, I tell you! The man had diabetes for a long time and refused insulin treatment! Mrs. Grosu was getting angry.

— No, I didn't hear that! I don't know. Now, you see, my sister really did die of COVID, poor thing!

— I heard about it! My deepest condolences, Mrs. Aludean. You must have been going through a hard time, and we neighbors didn't even know! Being cooped up in the house... Oh, oh! This pandemic seems to wipe out every trace of humanity. How did it happen?

— It went quickly. All the symptoms came on relatively

suddenly, and then, within a few hours, it was off to the hospital as if it had never even existed. I still can't believe it.

— Yeah, I know, I know what it's like to lose someone you love... Mrs. Grosu glanced briefly at Nelu, blushing brightly. If you need anything, just let me know, she offered. You were very kind and comforted me when my husband died.

'I tried to comfort her, but this Nelu seems to have succeeded better,' Amalia would have liked to comment.

— Yes, thank you. It's great to have such nice neighbors!

— Goodbye! said Mrs. Grosu finally.

— Goodbye! Nelu also said hello.

— Have a nice day! Goodbye, my dear ones.

— Pretty woman! wondered Nelu, after they had gone some distance.

— I never met a kinder, more forgiving person in my life. When her upstairs neighbor flooded her, she refused his money on the ground that he had a bigger mess, and that, having children, he needed money much more than she did. Now tell me, how many would do that?

— Not many! I, for one, certainly wouldn't! admitted Nelu. Who's wrong, must pay!

And she came to take care of my husband when I had to go left and right... And, look, I wasn't able to repay him when his sister got sick! I didn't even know she died. I found out later.

— Don't worry. You would have been if you'd known! Did she live with her sister? Nelu inquired.

— No. I mean, yes. Malvina came from America at the end of February. She came to stay with her sister in her old age! But you know what I find strange? Before Malvina came, I had never heard Mrs. Aludean say anything about her sister. In fact, I didn't even know she had a sister!

— Well, maybe the conversation didn't get started.

— Now, come to think of it, Mrs. Aludean didn't talk much about herself, even though I told her all about myself... Malvina, her sister, was more talkative. Well, as far as I could tell, it wasn't long after she came that the pandemic set in, and they put us behind walls and kept us from meeting. This Malvina struck me as a little hotheaded. The easy-going type, if you know what I mean... She was like the opposite of Mrs. Aludean. Sisters, but nothing alike!

And it didn't seem to me that she was showing any concern for Mrs. Amalia. Then why would she want to spend her old age with her?

— Well, with an American pension, you can live here like a king! Perhaps she thought of her sister's loneliness and material deprivation. But didn't these old ladies have children? wondered Nelu.

— Mrs. Aludean had a daughter, but she died. But that's what an acquaintance who worked with her on the fruit farm told me. She never mentioned the girl, and I never thought to ask her... so as not to bother the dead. And I never asked Mrs. Malvina. I assumed not, since she'd come to spend her old age with her sister.

— Maybe she just got homesick. That never dies! Roots never die! he concluded.

— Yes, maybe... Still, that Malvina woman is the true embodiment of the devil, believe me. Even her eyes didn't look right. I thought she was so gorgeous. If she'd been a little younger, I think I'd have said she was frivolous... But for the dead, all the best. I think Mrs. Amalia loved her very much. I just didn't feel the feeling was mutual, and I found it odd that they hadn't seen each other since they were young.

— Well, to each his own. Sometimes, brothers are so

different.

  — See, that's what I don't understand, Nelu, darling. Raised in the same environment by the same parents, they have the same blood and when they become adults, they forget all the pride of their childhood, as if that would not even bond them... I really don't understand why they say that "blood is thicker than water" because I don't really see it that way!

  — You don't understand because you were an only child, but look, I guess I didn't tell you, I haven't talked to my brother in like three years either. We're so different. I'm too stubborn, he's just looking out for himself. That's what happens to all broods that leave the nest. They stay on their own.

Chapter 3

Amalia steps into the apartment. She still found the silence inside odd. She hung up her coat and noticed that her fingers began to tremble. Not because of the investigation. At least from that point of view, she wasn't particularly concerned. Instead, she was afraid of that sensation of panic that she had experienced in the past, which, once overcome, left her feeling weak and with immense pain in her soul. Over time, she slowly learned to ignore it, trying to imagine that her daughter, Lili, was still alive, somewhere far away, across the ocean. Then, she came to believe it.

Malvina's arrival changed everything in Amalia's life. She was aware of the pain and the loss, and the need to see Lili again only resulted in the despair of helplessness.

"I was driving." Malvina's words, confessed at the moment between life and death, insidiously wormed their way into every synapse, threatening to become an obsession. They poisoned her soul.

She went to the refrigerator to open a bottle of milk. After today, she didn't feel like cooking anything. She was exhausted. Sitting in her armchair, she turned on the TV. They announced the number of infected, the number of deaths in the country. She imagined the grief in the souls of people who had lost a loved one, but at least that grief was no longer hers, it seemed distant. People became numbers and were lost in statistics. Despite the period of isolation and the restrictions imposed, the hospitals were full of the sick, and the plague was still spreading like a dangerous enemy, attacking relentlessly, coming out of nowhere and spreading terror. The voice of the announcers, in tone and in the countless breaking news bulletins – which interrupted every television broadcast – warned the population of imminent catastrophe. It seemed as if the Apocalypse was approaching, as if the Wheel of Life itself was slowing down, heralding the approach of the end of the world.

The fact that she had learned from Mrs. Grosu that Mr. Pantelimon on the third floor, diagnosed with this miserable COVID-19, had been admitted to the ICU ward affected her more than she let on. Could she end up like that? How long would you be safe from this virus without contracting it? There were asymptomatic people. Maybe God will take care of her. God who? If he really exists, he's been avoiding her all her life... A lost sheep she'd forgotten. Unloved by anyone, not even God. Only Lili had loved her, she had no doubt about that, but even she had left her...

Why would she want to go so far away? Here she had her... Did Lili ever realize how she broke her heart then?

They had each other, and it wasn't easy to overcome the material hardships, but above all the prejudices of people in a small provincial town, and not once had Amalia thought of moving elsewhere. She could see the disapproval in others' eyes, even when they spoke kindly to her. She felt stigmatized even at work, even though her professional expertise was often sought by colleagues or even her bosses. However, when she left the perimeter of the workplace, she became almost a stranger to them. If she happened to meet her colleagues on the street, they would greet her with a tip of their lips, eyes downcast. But Amalia didn't miss her friends, preferring to stay away from the world. After all, even as a child, things had been like that.

While Amalia endured the reactions of those around her with stoicism, Lili did not. The little girl would often come home crying from school, asking her questions that Amalia did not want to answer. The children openly showed their mockery. They could be very mean, and Lili suffered. She hadn't enjoyed the presence of a friend either.

— Mom, Dana told me that her grandparents on her mother's

side are called Matei, not Zamfir, like her. Why are my grandparents still called Aludean, like us?

Aludean is an old, traditional name, my dear, Amalia replied.

– Today, Mia was brought to school by her father. She was very proud! Mommy, where's my daddy? Shouldn't I have a father? Lili asked her some other time.

– My love for you is so great that no one else's love could last. We have each other and we're very proud of it!

– Yes, but I'd still like to meet him someday...

– You can't, darling, he's dead...

Amalia realized that her wounds were only seemingly healed from how easily they opened. She also felt a burden of guilt for her little girl. An unseen hand seemed to transfer some of the unhappiness of the Aludean women, prolonging an ill fate from one generation to the next. If only she were able to free herself from this pain! But she couldn't! She simply couldn't!

Gradually, Lili learned to stop asking her mother awkward questions, sensing her hidden suffering, and she responded to the offenses of her classmates in her own way, striving to do better than them. And she succeeded!

Only one episode darkened her adolescence. She had fallen in love. It was the first time she kept secrets from her mother. It had ended badly. She gave in to the boy's insistence on intimacy, and he bragged to others about their exploits. Lili found this out unexpectedly when a classmate unexpectedly asked her to sleep with him.

– Why would I do that? We're not friends, I don't love you! replied Lili startled.

– Come on, forget it! We all know you're a whore. Besides, you're your mother's daughter, aren't you?

She had no idea where she got the strength to beat the young man so hard, even though he was a head taller and stronger than she was. The incident was brought to the attention of the headmistress and Amalia was called in to report the situation. If things had calmed down at the school management level, the same could not be said for the atmosphere among the students. Her classmates no longer dared to insult Lili, but instead isolated her, rarely saying a word to her.

The girl's departure from Lugoj to Bucharest, far away from the provincial gossip and animosity of those around her, following her admission to the Faculty of Letters, was fortunate. Amalia, however, felt lonely, unable to protect her daughter from whatever vices her life had shown her. She called Lili several times a day to make sure she was all right and went as often as she could to visit her. She repeated to herself that this was the law of nature, that a child has once grown takes its own life into its own hands, but she could not help feeling that part of her body was being torn away, that her very being was being scattered into a thousand pieces. After graduation, Lili told her she was staying in the capital city. She had taken a low-paid job at a newspaper, but seemed convinced that this was the beginning of a successful career. She was so idealistic! So naive! She soon realized that she couldn't publish anything, that there were people she was not allowed to "bother," that she had to respect the political orientation of the newspaper... She soon found herself disappointed and frustrated. She had otherwise dreamed of her profession and was well aware that she could achieve more. She envisioned free journalism, "like abroad," without questioning the fact that, as long as you are paid by someone, a journalist is not really free anywhere.

Lili decided to leave, letting herself be carried away by the American illusion, where "any dream can come true," but above all, by the promises Malvina had made to her when she returned home for the first time since she had fled the country.

Amalia was devastated, as if she had never had the right to love. Even that love had been taken from her... It was the first time she thought that it was not she who had protected her daughter, but her daughter who had looked after her, for the feeling of love Amalia had for her was beyond everything, beyond hatred, away from pain...

And now she wondered how she had survived so much drama.

She'd always had to take care of herself to get through somehow... "She, with the power of thought," she told to herself, but this expression that Malvina sometimes made her even more upset.

She turned off the TV and, with some hesitation, picked up the novel that Malvina had read just before the first symptoms of her illness appeared. He had never touched any of her work before. She took a long look at the title: "The Right to Forgiveness," written by an author she didn't know about. Here you are! What a title! Malvina hadn't finished reading it, and the page she reached was bent at the top corner. Amalia found it strange to be reading now what her sister had read not so long ago. She had the unnatural feeling that by simply taking a look, by reading to the very end of the book, she would take over her sister's life and carry it forward. It was silly, of course, but she couldn't get rid of it.

Something fell on the floor. It was a small, old photograph, black and white and yellow with age. For a moment, her heart stopped. It was the three of them, her, Malvina and Dorian. Oh, yes! She knew exactly when it was taken! How could she forget such a thing? But she couldn't remember ever seeing it.

The camera had captured the moment for posterity, a token of passing through that space and that moment. That's all, nothing remains after a hectic life, full of events, experiences, and feelings.

Of the three people photographed at the time, two were no longer there... Only she, Amalia, still overshadowed the earth... He focused on Malvina's face. It wasn't Malvina's beauty that struck her, but the living energy that had managed to transcend the photographic film.

Slightly slanted eyes, a mouth larger than would have fit into any beauty standard - nothing was perfect, but at 18, her sister was bursting with vitality. The photograph doesn't capture that particular shade of her eyes, coppery with greenish iridescence. By contrast, she, Amalia, the one with the perfect oval shape of the face, the lips and nose that could have been a model for any portrait painter, looked... so... washed out! A washed-out blonde with small, sunken eyes of a pale blue that in the black and white picture had turned a cold gray, she seemed devoid of any youthful charm.

She looked intently, with mingled feelings, at the young man who was embracing both of them around the waist. Dorian! He looked at Malvina in a way... How? Amalia asked herself. In a way, he had never looked at her... The picture was taken in the village of Vultureni. That's where the disaster had begun.

This was the very picture she had chosen to put between the pages of her book! Why? She was convinced he had done it deliberately to be discovered by her at some point. So very her! And Amalia labeled it cynicism. Malvina... Malvina... continued to hurt her even posthumously, Amalia concluded.

Chapter 4

Dorian was a year older than her, the kind of young man who was attractive, cheerful, always with a good joke in his pocket, seeming to take all of life in jest. He never tackled personal or serious discussions and had become, perhaps for that very reason, the life of any party. Brown-haired, blue-eyed, with generous eyebrows and an athletic body, he was compared by the young girls to Alain Delon, the actor who had won all the beauty contests of their generation. Girls were sighing, falling in love, attracted like a magnet. Although the protruding chin showed determination and a certain sternness, the mischievous, slightly ironic smile softened the impression. He was well aware of his charm, considering himself irresistible, but in front of the opposite sex, he avoided showing his arrogance. Thanks to his intuition, he knew exactly what to say to each young woman, giving her not only what she wanted to hear, but, above all to listen - a skill he called a true art, as he boasted among friends. Thus, even the most demanding girls, with all the credulity of youth, saw him as the perfect man.

The competition between them for Dorian's attention was also a source of envy, but it is no less true that the boys often experienced the same feeling, seeing the success their colleagues enjoyed among the female students. Dorian was considered a Don Juan of the Polytechnic, a charmer from whom they could learn a lot about women. Some tried to imitate him, taking on his joking air, others waited patiently to see who would be the next "victim" left behind and tried to be the first to comfort her.

Amalia met Dorian at a party organized in a dorm room by one of her classmates, Ema. Although she too had been a victim of Dorian's charms, she posed in his presence, trying to show that she was not affected by their break-up nor surprised that it had happened so soon after they had become acquainted with each other's physical intimacies, but secretly hoping to win him back. Amalia, far too sober and serious, was not the most pleasant presence, so she was rarely invited to any of the parties organized by her colleagues. At 23, still in her final year of Biology, she could count on one hand the parties she had gone to. What bad luck that she had gone to exactly the one! Amalia wasn't used to rock'n'roll music, which she found too hard, preferring the ballads. So she planned to stay for an hour and then retire to the quiet of her home. Anyway, she didn't know the steps, she didn't have the grace to dance, even if she had tried to practice in front of the mirror, in the privacy of her room. Malvina would have laughed if she had caught her!

Besides, most of the girls already had boyfriends, which was another reason for her discomfort. She poured herself a glass of beer, so as not to give the impression that she didn't fit in with the cheerful atmosphere around her, clutching the glass, savoring the hoppy liquor as if she had found in it a miracle. When the bitterness of the drink sickened him, he went to look out of the window, seemingly interested in the wind in the student campus.

— You don't seem to like this music...

Amalia winced. She turned, surprised to see Dorian approaching her.

— Really? Not really. Too much noise.

— I see.

— Do you like it?

— Honestly? Yes! he smiled back.

Dorian turned and shouted to one of the young men who had brought the tape recorder.

— Hey, Neluțu, put on some quieter music, like blues. Hey, we must respect everyone's tastes, right? After all, we want everyone to have a good time!

Neluțu complied, finding a slow tune. Dorian took Amalia's

glass of beer from her hand, put it down, and then drew her gently towards him, dancing.

— Do you like that? he asked.

— It works.

— It just works? he laughed.

— Yes, it does.

— What's your name? I'm sorry, I didn't catch your name when we introduced ourselves...

— We didn't introduce ourselves, but we can do it now. I'm Amalia!

— Nice name. Lia, Ama, Ami, Amo..., what do people spoil you? Dorian asked.

— People don't spoil me, she replied dryly.

— May I call you by your name? I'll call you Amo, for love! whispered the young man. His voice took on a special tone of mystery.

— What's your name? she asked.

Dorian grinned, thinking the girl was joking. Then, seeing that she was as serious as she could be, he was puzzled. He didn't think there was a girl on campus who didn't know him! And the girls in biology or philology were his favorites. On the other hand, he'd never seen her before, either, even though he pretended to know all of Emma's classmates. And yet...

— Dorian, he introduced himself.

— And your name is beautiful. Very nice. It comes from longing, she flirtatiously returned his reply, also surprised by her own boldness.

Dorian welcomed her words as an invitation and joined her body to his, and Amalia bit her lips so as not to admit that she felt as if she had waited a lifetime for this moment.

She didn't even realize that her steps were naturally

following Dorian's, that she let herself be led by him to the music without hesitation. She was dancing! It was magic, but she tried not to show it. She almost gave herself away the moment Dorian pulled her gently away from him, pausing for a moment, watching her very intently.

— There's something... I don't know, something peculiar about you, he whispered in a deliberately hoarse voice.

— Are you trying to flirt with me?

— Ha, ha, ha! I think I am! Is it working? Dorian laughed at her reaction.

— No.

— Why not?

— Because I'm not a goose... I have a head on my shoulders and I use it. I know exactly how I am, for better or worse, Amalia replied, determined.

She couldn't imagine that anyone could like her, could appreciate her rather sober, silent nature. When she looked in the mirror, she thought she saw a wilted flower. No one sought her friendship, not even her own sister. She'd been that way as long as she could remember. Who could like her, when she didn't like herself much, and her own mother seemed to see only her faults?

As far as Dorian was concerned, she'd labeled him "unreliable," which was exactly the kind of boy she hated. After a couple of dances, when she decided to leave, too overwhelmed by the immediacy of finding herself in the good graces of such a charming boy, he offered to walk her home.

— Are you staying with the host? inquired Dorian.

— Why ask me that? Don't I have the look of a city girl?

— Not really, said Dorian.

— Why? she answered, surprised, though she suspected the answer.

— Because you're not nosy... You seem quiet and sweet-tongued. Mysterious.

— Mysterious? "I wouldn't say so," she commented, surprised that anyone should think so. Still, I'm from Bucharest. I live with my parents. I was born here, I grew up here, I want to stay here.

— I understand. I'm a country boy. I'm from Vultureni, but you probably haven't heard of the village. It's in Vâlcea. It's a great place, but once you get a taste of the city, there's no way I could imagine living in the country... In the same way, after almost five years in the capital, I can't see myself living in a provincial town. Everything is alive here, there's always something going on. It's full of youth and fun! When we finish university they'll give us assignments somewhere in the country, but I, for one, will do anything to come back to Bucharest.

— It may not be the most beautiful city in the world, but once you get used to it, it's hard to change it for another city, isn't it?

— It definitely has a special energy. From what I understand, you're a classmate of Ema... I've known her for a long time. So you're a biology student, too! How come I've never met you before?

— I don't really go to parties. I'm more of a studious type. Call me a nerd or a bookworm - I don't mind.

Amalia avoided admitting that she was rarely invited to one.

— Well, cleverness is good, and study, I don't say, but fun, dear Amo, is a state of mind! It adds color to life. And, after all, why not take advantage of youth? You know? I've heard some people say they fly. Ha! Ha! Dorian laughs.

— "What good is all this wisdom if we don't know how to enjoy it?" replied Amalia.

— You see? You've gotten my words fast!

— Not me, Cicero! In fact, you've come to Cicero's words. Not me. Look, I'd really rather go home now. Are you disappointed?

— A little. I'd have liked to have danced, talked, gotten to know each other better...

— Stay at the party, you'll be better off, believe me!

There's no need to drive me. I can handle it.

— How could I not? I couldn't let you walk alone through Bucharest at this hour! And I won't take no for an answer! I'm not the man to back down!

— Are... you?

— What?

— A man! Amalia was also surprised by her impertinence and thoughtlessness.

He put on a serious face. He gripped her chin firmly.

— You're not the type, so I wouldn't advise you not to live so much on the edge! he warned her.

Maybe the fuse had lit then. Perhaps at that moment, in a treacherous corner of her mind, the question "but what if?" was born. Maybe that's when she began to hope that someone in this world might love her too, the faded, charmless girl.

Amalia didn't have many pictures of her youth. She only kept the lonely ones from her childhood where she appeared alone. The few that had Malvina in them, she had burned as well as the ones of Dorian, as if the simple act of setting them on fire could have burned his own memories. No, but he had deluded herself. Seeing him again in this picture was heartbreaking, even all these years later. It stung. Some wounds leave ugly scars, hiding a rotting soul, and others can never heal, bleeding over and over.... Some people were better able to overcome life's troubles. Fallen down, they would pick themselves up off the ground, shake themselves off and move on. She envied them. She had never been able to do that, even though she'd always tried to appear strong, steadfast. The past pulled her back like chains hanging from her legs...

Chapter 5

Dorian had amazed all his friends with his preference for the serious and "nerdy" student, being often seen with her walking around Bucharest, going to the theater, and also to various student parties. If, at first, everyone was distrustful, believing that she was a fan of the famous "charmer," they gradually noticed that their bond was growing closer and closer, and the idea that opposites attract each other was taking shape in the minds of those who knew them.

As for Amalia, she was blossoming. She was slowly opening herself to a knowledge she had no idea could exist. This love still frightened her with its intensity, and she realized that if she and Dorian were to break up, the whole world would be different, changed, and mark her forever. This was the reason why she was putting off taking the decisive step, total dedication, more than her mother's advice, repeated obsessively to her daughters to remain chaste until marriage.

– Be careful, girls, don't let him come into your ease! Men only want to fulfill their instincts, and then they can leave you high and dry and knocked-up! And grass hardly grows on a trodden path!

Malvina laughed heartily when she heard it, but Amalia took it seriously, convinced of the accuracy of what she said. However, it wasn't the advice that made her hesitate, even though she had always tried her best to please her parents, but the certainty that her life would change later, and not for the better. She tried very hard to hide her feelings. The care she took over her dress, her diet, the way she looked, her more frequent outings on the town, the state of happiness that lit up her eyes and the smile that often broke out on a face used to being serious could hardly escape the observation of others.

– Listen, Malvina approached her one evening, "did you do it?"

– Did I do what? Amalia pretended not to understand.

– Well, you know, "let him come along at your ease," laughed Malvina, quoting her mother.

– With whom?

– Come on, come on, you're obviously in love! Who is it? Won't you introduce him to us? I'm dying to meet your lover!

– He's not that important to me, Amalia lied. I haven't gotten that far.

– I can't wait to see what he's like.

– Malvina, if mom could hear you, you'd see what a spanking you'd get!

– Listen, promise you'll tell me what and how?

– When and if I did, I think you'd be the last person I'd tell!

The anger that came through these words silenced Malvina. After all, what could she expect from her sister? They had never been on the same wavelength, they had never reacted in the same way, they had never had the same concerns, too different from each other. They had never confided in each other because Amalia was too introverted and not willing to listen to her sister, cutting off from the start any communication on personal matters.

– Amalia goes out with a boy! she announces at dinner the next evening, Malvina.

If this had been met with distrust, the sudden flush on Amalia's cheeks was enough to give her away. In the silence of the dining-room, the cutlery on the table echoed.

– And why are we only now finding out?

Mom's accusing voice made Amalia swallow hard. She shot a glare at Malvina, much to her amusement.

– Uh... uh... nothing serious yet.

– Listen, Amalia, it's only serious when she puts the ring on your finger! Mom thundered, pounding her fist on the table.

– And even then! the father completes.

–You shut up," said his wife. Keep pouring your wine until you see double and stay out of it!

– Out! See two skirts? I have enough with one.

– With the power of thought, it will be okay! Malvina giggled.

Amalia wondered how her sister could react like that when their mother went out of her temper, but more importantly, how she was never scolded for it. No matter how silly things she did, her little sister was overlooked. Moreover, if she happened to be around, Amalia took all the blame and punishment. When Malvina made a mistake, her mother's tone was lenient, almost bland, while when she scolded Amalia, her voice vibrated with displeasure. She wondered why parents showed younger children more kindness. Why does the eldest always have to give in?

But in time, she came to realize that it wasn't just the mother's more indulgent attitude towards her youngest child. It was more than that! He had the feeling that she was unloved, and with time, as the years went by, this feeling grew into conviction. Amalia had been more internalized, but over time, she became an increasingly sullen child as she inhibited her rebellion more and more... She never knew what she had done wrong to her mother. He tried his best to please her, waiting for praise that never came... Mr. Aludean, the father, was most of the time silent and joking, becoming humorous and ironic only when he let himself be at Bachus' mercy, sometimes having a glass more than usual. It didn't happen often because, most of the time, he didn't feel like putting up with his wife's pain. He was too little involved in raising the girls, considering it a "woman's job" and that his only duty was to work to bring in the money his family needed. He left the impression that his daughters were just creatures that bore his name, a sort of appendage to a house he owned. However, he behaved identically towards his daughters, unlike their mother, Mrs. Cornelia Aludean, who made no effort to hide the fact that of the two daughters, the younger, Malvina, was his favorite. Besides, Amalia felt that she was an unwanted child and that she didn't have the qualities that would make her loveable.

Chapter 6

The doorbell rang insistently, dispelling her memories for the moment. She put the picture back in the book, planning to burn it later. She looked somewhat fearfully through the peephole and saw Agatha. He didn't feel like her right now, but it was preferable to see her than the police or the prosecutor's office. When he opened the door, he managed to put on a very welcoming smile.

– Kisses, Agatha. You haven't changed your habit. You never announce when you're coming. What if I wasn't home?

– If you weren't, then you weren't and full stop. A walk at this age is necessary, after all, otherwise I risk ankylosing. But no kiss? Agatha stretched out her cheek, her lips curling up in a pout.

– Agatha, it's pandemic. I don't want to give you a virus. Have you forgotten that Malvina died of COVID?

– Yes, don't tell me! Who knows what disease she had? Listen to me, I'm older than you! This is a figment. This virus doesn't exist, dear! They've got some dirty plans for mankind, it's all too neatly stitched up!

– They who?

– The ones who run the world.

– Maybe they do and that's why they invented this virus. If my own sister hadn't died right here in front of me, I might even be tempted to believe it didn't exist... But people are dying because of it. Look, my neighbor Pantelimon, I don't know if you've met him, but he was taken to the Emergency service with COVID, in serious condition.

– How could I not know him? The one who keeps spying when people enter the block, he was a butcher. But he's old, dear, what do you expect at his age?

Amalia doesn't comment. She would have liked to remind Agatha how old she was, that she was over 80, that her neighbor

Pantelimon was younger than her by a significant difference of years. But she thought that there was no point in changing the woman's self-perception if she was happy with herself. Perhaps Agatha was anchored in a time known only to herself, and Amalia suspected it was her way of running away from the idea of old age, of denying the obvious.

— Will you have tea? Amalia changed the subject.

— How about a glass of plum juice? Like this, as a throat disinfectant... Kills any germs.

— It does. I'd serve you food, but I haven't cooked anything today. I have some pretzels if you want.

— 'Excellent, my dear,' Agatha replied as she leaned her cane against the edge of her chair and sat down with some difficulty at the table.

Although Agatha was only seven years older than Amalia, she was Amalia's aunt, the younger sister of Cornelia Aludean, Amalia's mother. She was his sister only after her father's second marriage.

Their childhood relationship had been almost non-existent, as neither Amalia's grandmother, deserted by her adulterous husband, nor Agatha's mother had encouraged their visits. Agatha later married a man in Timişoara, where she moved to follow her husband.

Long after she settled in Lugoj, Amalia did not look for Agatha, even though they lived so close to each other. The closeness of their distance failed to soften the coldness of their relationship. As a result, Amalia didn't look for her mother's sister for long - she found it hard to call her aunt. She avoided any acquaintance, any relationship, preferring to manage on her own. After all, the world hadn't shown her much kindness!

Things changed the year her father died. It is said that trouble never comes alone, and the Aludeans seemed to be living up to this saying. That same year, Cornelia had a stroke. She escaped with her life, but she was left with after-effects. She was slower to speak, had difficulty pronouncing certain words, and moved slowly, losing her balance slightly. Amalia felt compelled to bring her mother to Lugoj. At first, Cornelia didn't even want to hear. After she fell and fractured her femur, which kept her bedridden for a long time, she had no choice. He accepted it as a must, but only after getting Amalia to promise to have Mr. Aludean's grave moved to Lugoj.

– He was a good man, raised you, worked for his family... He was a good father to you... If I go to Lugoj and die there, what will it be like? Me buried in one place, him in another... No way...

Amalia had kept her promise.

As fate would have it, Agatha's husband died soon after. The two widows now had something to bring them closer. Agatha made a habit of visiting them regularly, often staying overnight.

– I like Lugoj. It's a quiet, pleasant city, not like Timișoara.

The thought of moving to Lugoj took shape in Agatha's mind. She had left her son her apartment in Timișoara and with the money she had left the deceased, she had bought a cozy little house in the small market town.

Agatha and Cornelia Aludean had dominating personalities and resembled each other in their way of being, so that the late friendship forged between them was surprising to those who knew them, including Amalia.

Agatha was now very wrinkled, slightly bent forward, leaning on her cane, but she was not giving up her poppy-colored lipstick or the striking reddish tint to her hair, but who would dare to judge the tastes of an 83-year-old woman?

– My sweetheart! What bad luck! Perhaps you're under the illusion that you'll be together in your old age... that you could renew the relationships you'd broken for so long... God had other plans...

— It wasn't easy. I'd just gotten used to the idea of having someone to talk to... I always thought I'd go first. That would have been natural.

— It would have. God must have mixed up your fates. Listen, I still don't understand why Malvina came back to the country after all this time! She didn't even come to her own mother's funeral! If I were you, I wouldn't have received her.

— Well, she's my sister, what could I do? She was... whatever. And then... the ocean... the great distance...

— Nonsense! Agatha waved her hand. She broke your mother's heart! Cornelia adored her. Well, Malvina's always been a bit of a wild one, as far as I know. Naughty, that's what your mother called her when she was little.

— Yes, my mother adored her, indeed!

— And yet, Malvina hasn't visited her mother since she got sick! That's something! At least dropping her a bone, so she'd have something for her trouble because they know she worked for good money, unlike us.

— Do we know how much trouble and problems our immigrants go through over there? They have to adapt, find jobs... Most of them don't leave for the good they have here. They all tell us they're doing well there, but...

They don't. It was too painful for her. She lowered her eyelids, trying to hide her bitterness. Agatha didn't seem to realize it.

— Let the immigrants wait until I feel sorry for them! she continued, unmoved. Let them come back if it's so hard for them, she tapped her pointing finger on the table. I say that those who run away are cowards. They should've stayed in the country and fought so they'd be better off here. They shouldn't just go off around the world and leave the country to bastards and bastards. From the sidelines, it's easy to talk and give advice. But who's going to fight, darling, here with all these bastards, these crooks who run us? Me, in the cane?

It was only then that she realized that her words were twisting a knife in Amalia's open wound.

– You see, I didn't mean to upset you. For the moment, I forgot about Lili... Oh, God!

She clenched Amalia's hand in her fist with crooked, gnarled fingers.

– Agatha, you haven't done anything wrong. Lili shouldn't have gone... She had my love here. It wasn't enough.

– It's the plum brandy. She opened my mouth more than she should have.

– Another drink? Amalia asked, more out of a desire to change the subject and switch the conversation to another frequency.

– Yes, but go on, have one, because this one disinfects the head, with all the memories, not just the throat.

Okay, come on, I'll please you, even though I don't like plum brandy at all and I can't understand how anyone could.

– You don't know what's good! Why do you keep those yew twigs in your coffer? Didn't you hear it's poisonous?

– It has beautiful flowers. Taxus baccata, that's the scientific name, Amalia told her with a knowing air.

– God, you shot me! laughed Agatha. You know, dear, you studied biology. Cheers!

– Cheers!

Agatha sipped her drink at leisure, disdaining the tradition of drinking from a fire. For a while they let the silence between them settle in, both meditating, one on the problems that were troubling her, the other on the flavor of the plum brandy.

— Agatha, have you any idea why my mother didn't love me? Amalia broke the silence.

— What nonsense are you talking about? How could your mother not love you?

— No, she didn't, said Amalia in a clinical tone. No matter how hard I tried to please her, no matter how hard I tried to please her... I couldn't.

— Damn, what happened to you? At 76, complaining that your mother didn't love you! Is that so? Darling, either Malvina's death has affected you too much, or you're getting sclerotized. You know, I'm always praying she'll keep my mind in one piece for as many days as I have.

— Well, it doesn't affect me now, but as a child, I often wondered, and after Malvina left, and after father died, when mother came to live with me, I kept wondering... You know, it had crossed my mind as a child that maybe I wasn't her child, that maybe she had adopted me, or maybe she had to marry my father because she was pregnant and maybe I had another father?

Agatha looked at her pointedly.

— You'd better gulp down that glass of brandy to make your life more 'drinkable.' What a bad habit to disturb the dead!

— Well, perhaps you're right that Malvina's death affected me. I don't know why I brought it up now! Amalia was sorry she'd brought it up.

— She never confided in me.

— Yes, she wasn't the type, but I thought... how you've become friends over the years...

— 'But I know from my father,' continued Agatha, surprising Amalia, 'that poor Cornelia, your mother, went through a great trouble.... It was at the height of the war in '44. Poverty, misery, deprivation... The bombing started. They sent Cornelia to the countryside, to Răscruci, to some relatives, thinking that she might be safer there than in Bucharest... Except that the Russians invaded, leaving disasters behind them... Those were the times... Big trouble... Young Cornelia... You know what I mean... I heard she had a hard time recovering from the rape. Her father then found a man to take her like that, knocked her up... and married her. She found Aludean, a fine boy, but poor. Good man, he didn't make the difference between you and Malvina...

Amalia was shocked to hear that, although she herself had suggested the idea. But she had never seriously considered the possibility. After all this time! What a secret so sacredly guarded all these years, only to burst out of Agatha's mouth as easily as if she had said it was raining outside! And how many things in the past could now be at least partially explained.

– As for her marriage, Agatha continued, he was exactly the husband Cornelia would have wanted. I think she was satisfied in the end. He brought the money at home, he wasn't wandering about, and he never interfered in her decisions! He still liked a drink, but not too much, and when he happened to get a little tipsy, he became quite likeable.

– Yes, probably, Amalia replied, more to say something.

– But I think your mother loved you... In her own way. You were a good girl, always obedient, serious, going to college...

– "You're wrong, Agatha," Amalia contradicted her in a more heated tone. She couldn't get over the pain of seeing her beloved daughter - and it wasn't me - run away! "And she blamed me for it!" she added in thought.

– Do I know what to say? It's more convenient to look for the guilty elsewhere than in oneself. You see, in the last years of her life, we got closer, but the truth is that I told her everything while she talked very little about herself or about you. It was like something strange keeping her from talking. She was suffering in silence... But one thing I know for sure. That she was afraid that her unhappiness would follow you, you, Malvina and even her granddaughters, when she told me this, I reassured her that it was not possible, that each person is unique in his or her own way and that times are not always the same... And I also know for sure that what happened to Lili affected her deeply. I think it also hastened Cornelia's end... But you can't change man's fate and God's work. It's best not to dwell on the past. We won't be prisoners of it as long as life goes on! What's the use? The dead with the dead, the living with the living! Put some more "disinfectant" in my glass, dear, for you've reminded me of sad things. Come on, let me wash them a little more.

Amalia complied. She'd always been amused by Agatha's appetite for plum brandy, but she also appreciated the fact that she never got drunk, knowing her measure. Only this time, her words had gotten ahead of her, and she couldn't stop them.

— Listen, why don't you take some of Malvina's clothes to the church, so that her sins may be forgiven? Agatha asked.

— I was going to. I still can't get around to sorting her things. You know how it is...

— Yes, yes, I know. When you manage it, let me know so we can go together. Maybe you can reach his daughter, Marlene, in case she wants to come to the funeral. You haven't seen her yet?

— Uh, no, I haven't. I called from Malvina's cell, left a message... I don't know how to get in touch with her! I only know what Malvina told me about her... And what Lili once told me, Amalia sighed. Lili liked her very much! She adored her! But... it's been ages since then... I suppose my mother was up to date about their life, but she also knew that it was taboo, that I never wanted to hear about them again... My information now is that she lives in New York, works at a big accounting firm, and is divorced. And I have her phone number.

— Yeah, that's all I know. I have the feeling that mother and daughter didn't get along very well, but Malvina didn't tell me that, so I deduced it... I thought, like a man, that's why she had decided to come back to the country... If you have a child there, why would you want to go so far away? You see, Malvina talked about everything for everyone, but little about what she didn't want.

— Agatha, I didn't really think she wanted to stay permanently... There were times I thought she wanted her share of her parent's inheritance, but she never said a word about it! In any case, I have no idea why she came... I'm quite sure though, it's not because she missed me too much!

— Anyway, you should have a funeral in six weeks.

— Of course, I'll do it, even if it's not for sure at six weeks. Let the number of infected decrease a bit, it's really dangerous to walk in crowds now.

— Whatever, but I still don't believe this virus exists. You know, more people die of fear, insanity and dark thoughts than COVID-19!

"Bullshit," Amalia said to herself.

Most people die of grief on this earth."

Chapter 7

After Agatha left, Amalia slumped on the sofa, completely exhausted. She closed her eyes. How many things now had an explanation!

It often happens like that in life. One often plays out gloomy scenarios, but in the back of one's mind, there is still the hope that events will not turn out exactly as they have planned. On other occasions, people formulate alarmist theories, but they have a sliver of faith that they will never be realized. One suspects a threatening illness, but, in reality, hopes that its seriousness will not be confirmed.

Amalia was in a state of ideational imponderability, in which the reality she knew was no longer reality, and between truth and lie stood an equal sign, in which she had lost all hope. Agatha had a strange, inexplicable effect on her, awakening her to the reality of the world, bringing her face to face with the cruel truth, and the only person she did not resent for it! Perhaps Agatha's spontaneity was to blame, perhaps the fact that the meetings with her were brief and then Amalia could quickly take refuge in her delusion.... Agatha seemed to be the only being who accepted her, with all her imperfections...

Maybe she sympathized her? Hard to believe since she herself had difficulty understanding herself... Except that their meetings made her deeply sad, exhausted her, made her feel as if she was passing through a portal from one time to another, from one space to another, from her reality into their reality. And that exhausted her.

She would have stayed in this state for a long time if she hadn't heard a lot of hubbubs, shouting, scandal from the corridor of the landing and the stairs of the block. She approached the peephole, but didn't see much. She opened the door slightly at about the same time as Mrs. Grosu, also alerted by the noise.

The upstairs neighbor, a single, divorced woman with two children, was shouting his head off.

– Don't take me anywhere! I have no one to leave the kids with! Nooo! Ow! Noooo!

– We're taking you to the hospital! It's an order and you'll have to obey it! another voice.

– Mommy! Mommy!" screamed the lady's little boy.

Where are they taking you?

– Mommy, don't leave us! whimpered the little girl.

Amalia climbed the stairs with an enviable sprint for her age. Two men dressed completely in white, like two cosmonauts, were dragging the upstairs girl towards a solitary confinement in the corridor of the landing while she resisted, holding on to everything in her path: the doorframe, the philodendron in the hallway, a bedside table that had been dropped by a tenant... A burly policeman, hiding his double chin behind an improperly

worn mask, watched the scene, waiting for the woman to be put in the solitary van.

– Mr. Policeman, you can't take her without caring that she has two children left alone! They're small children. The little boy has just turned 12 and the little girl six! said Mrs. Grosu afired.

– You'd better get on with your work and go down to your apartment unless you want us to consider you as an infected!

– Moooom! Moomyy!

– What's going on in here? A nurse, also dressed in white, came running up the stairs. Amalia recognized her voice. It was the same nurse who had come when she had called 911 to say Malvina was in a very serious condition.

– Lady, this woman is alone with two small children. What will happen to them if you take her? Mrs. Grosu, who was in the corridor one floor down, also interfered.

— The lady was a COVID infected at work, she was given a quick test, came out positive and was taken to hospital. That's all she had to do: wait for the PCR result! But no, she thought she was smart and ran away! Now, she has to bear the consequences! She will also be criminalized for knowingly endangering the health of others. That's it: you reap what you sow!

— But it's absurd! Of course, she ran away! Can't you see she has young children? insists Amalia, horrified by the authorities' reaction.

— Absurd or not, we have orders to take her, the policeman raises his voice. Come on, stop blabbering. Put her in the solitary van!

The two masked men forced her into a solitary van. The children were crying, screaming desperately at their mother.

— We'll take care of the little ones, don't be afraid,' Amalia tried to reassure the woman who was suffocating from pneumonia, fever, crying and despair.

— You can't, or you'll become 'infected', explains the nurse, addressing Mrs. Grosu. Children may be negative, but they are still infected! We notify the relevant institutions! We'll notify social welfare, let them deal with it.

— Just like you notified them when you hospitalized the mother? argued Mrs. Grosu, putting her hands on her hips. And how does that come about, to stay together in the same house, the mother hugs her babies, even kisses them, but some come out positive and others negative? Huh? Why don't you explain that to me?

— Consider us infected, but we can't leave the little ones in the lurch. We don't leave the house for days... Big deal. Amalia jumped to her neighbor's aid, her voice throaty with indignation.

— Oh, I know you! I was here when your sister got sick with

COVID or whatever it was, it didn't look like a viral infection! I saw it!

Amalia felt curled up inside. A cold chill ran down her spine, despite the fact that she was beginning to sweat. What had that nurse seen?

— How many COVID cases I've had the opportunity to go to, gee! the nurse continued in the same tone. Come on, stay out of it! Go quickly into your apartment and let us do our job! We're not here to waste time! the nurse shouted at Amalia.

— What's wrong? burst out Mrs. Grosu. How dare you talk like that to an old person who could be your mother? Have you no shame? Are you brainwashed? God forbid!

— Get out of the way! Let us through! he said firmly, warning Mrs. Aludean and Mrs. Grosu with a glance.

She spent the whole afternoon with Mrs. Grosu and her two children.

— Miserable! Filthy! To leave those children alone, without caring! And still that bitch insinuates that you didn't do what was necessary for your sister! These are not people, I tell you. They're monsters! It's like they're cloned by robots. Because with all the things they invent.

— You're right, you're right, Amalia replied absently. Her thoughts lingered on the threat in the nurse's eyes.

— Can I call Nelu to tell him to call here when he arrives?

— Of course, you can. Does he have to come?

— Uh, yes. Uh-huh. You know, a lot of people criticized me for finding someone so soon after my husband died. Maybe that's why we've avoided showing up together. Neither my children nor his are at peace with the situation and criticize us...

— I think you should ignore everyone. Do what your heart tells you. Nobody lives your life but you! Only you count and if you feel that something makes you happy, go ahead with your head held high, without caring what that person says.... or that...

The remembrance of Malvina's words, spontaneously appearing on her lips, seemed strange, unpleasant and unhappy to Amalia. Why had Malvina's words just now come into her mind?

— 'You are a very understanding person, unlike some people,' Mrs. Grosu answered gratefully.

— If you call Mr. Nelu, ask him to stop and get some chocolate and cookies for these children. It's on me.

— You're also a very generous person! You rarely meet good people these days. The world's growing older, don't you see? The more precious are the good ones that still exist! Yesterday, I went to the neighbor downstairs to return the screwdriver she lent me and she wouldn't even open the door! Can you imagine? She talked to me from behind the door. This pandemic's got us out of our minds, I swear! It's alienating people among themselves. Doesn't it seem to you that the world is becoming worse, more selfish, more insane? I wouldn't be surprised if there's a big war with this world gone mad!

— Well, not everybody. Look, you and me, for example... Come on, little ones, let's go find a cartoon film. What's your name? Dănuț?

— Yes, actually my name's Bogdan, but my mum calls me Dănuț, the little boy explained.

— And what's your little sister's name? asked Mrs Aludean, looking more towards the little girl this time.

— Elena, but we call her Neli.

— Sweetie, 'Amalia said to the little girl,' I'll bring you my doll from when I was little, the only one I have kept as a keepsake, will you?

— Yes..., the girl replied. Her bottom lip was still curled up, looking ready to burst into tears again. However, the woman's proposal caught her attention. At six, she still liked dolls.

– What's the doll's name?

– Lili... Actually, Lili Marlene... You know, there was a famous song... Wait a minute, let me look her up!

– But why is her neck broken? She was surprised when Amalia returned with the doll. She was about to cry again.

– Well, my sister and I pulled it once and the fabric broke a bit. Time then destroyed it...

– Can't we take her to the doctor and get her neck stitched back up?

– I can do it. Look, I'm going right now to find a needle and thread, and after I fix it, I'll give it to you as a present. At my age, I don't play with dolls anymore...

– Hooray! The little girl clapped her hands.

The child's joy reminded Amalia of another child who, many years ago, had also received a doll...

Chapter 8

Amalia had received the doll for her birthday. She had wanted a doll all her childhood. She'd always been told the family's little money was for food, not luxuries. It wasn't uncommon to see poverty creep into their lives and the lives of those she knew. He didn't even insist, using rags he'd gathered in clumps, drawing a nose, a mouth and two eyes on them with a lump of charcoal, wrapping them with another rag and imagining they were dolls. But when Malvina turned 4, her parents gave her a real doll, and Amalia still remembers the thrill, the pang of envy she felt when she saw Malvina jumping for joy with the doll in her arms.

A year later, on her 10th birthday, Amalia plucked up the courage to ask for a doll for her birthday.

– What do you need a doll for at this age? A book, yes, I understand. But, doll? You should learn, not to play with dolls! her mum hurried. Amalia's frustration showed itself in the eyes of Malvina's beautiful doll, which was the occasion for a long cry.

She had finally got the doll she had longed for. It wasn't bought from the toy shop like Malvina's, it didn't stand upright and didn't turn its head, but was knitted and stuffed with sponge inside. Still, it was beautiful, it was special. And it was hers. She named her Lili Marlene, inspired by a song her mother hummed. Amalia used to hold her to her chest when she went to bed at night and put her with her at the little table when she studied.

– Since they gave you the doll, you haven't spoken to me! whimpered Malvina.

There was some reason for her complaint, because Amalia's affections were directed solely towards Lili Marlene.

After a period of aversion, Malvina decided to play with the doll, copying her big sister's gestures, and the slap she received from her big sister when she was surprised, made her run to her mother to complain.

— Mummy, Amalia beat me!

— What? Why did she do that?

— For playing with her doll! But I let her play with my dolls and I didn't beat her!

Perhaps the girl's tears, perhaps the fact that she noticed that her eldest daughter was showing an abnormal passion for her age for that doll, made Mrs Aludean call Amalia to 'report' and bite her.

— That's it! Right now you give the doll to Malvinas. Is that clear?

— No, I'm not! I won't give it to her! She's mine! I got it!

— Shame on you! How dare you contradict me? The palm resounded on Amalia's cheek, reddening it.

Amalia didn't say a word. She looked at Malvina hatefully and threw the doll on the floor.

Days passed without Amalia showing any sign that she was still interested in the doll, even though Malvina often came to tempt her, waving it under her nose.

— Do you want it?

Amalia didn't answer, just put on a superior air.

— I wouldn't give it to you anyway!

But one night, after making sure that everyone in the house was asleep, she took the doll and went into the kitchen. He stroked it, held it to his chest.

— Better dead if you can't be mine!

She patiently cut her 'neck' to the side, just enough to stop her head from hanging upright. The threads were hanging where she'd cut.

— You don't have to cut on the other side, after all. You're dead anyway, she whispered to the doll.

A noise interrupted her. She pricked his ears to see where it was coming from. She realised she had caught a mouse in the trap her mother had improvised from an upside-down jar propped on its side on half a walnut. She was sick of mice. She saw it spinning madly inside the jar, looking for a way to escape, but finding none.

– Little mouse, I'll do a good deed, she whispered.

She picked up the threads on the table, put the knife back. She approached the jar, lifted it up a little, waited for the wriggling mouse to turn round, and then suddenly grabbed it by the tail, holding it as tightly as she could, despite the rodent's desperate protests. He quickly placed the mouse in Malvinas's toy box. She then silently went back into the kitchen, retrieved the "deceased" Lili Marlene and, arriving back in the bedroom, slipped her back inside, lifting the lid just a little, fearfully.

She wasn't present the next morning for her little sister's fright when the little sister, finally free at last, leapt out of the toy box, nor for the hysteria caused by the discovery of the doll with its neck cut in half, its head lolling to one side and its strings hanging out. Amalia only caught the exchange at dinner in the evening and deduced what had happened.

– If the mouse gnawed it, I don't need it! Malvina complained to her mother.

– Throw it away, sighed Mrs Aludean in exasperation. I'll buy you a new doll when I can.

Amalia took it out of the rubbish bin and hid it in an old trunk in the attic.

No-one blamed her. But in Mum's eyes, she saw suspicion and bitterness, but who knows? Maybe that's how she saw it. Maybe it just seemed that way. With the passing of so many years, even the most important memories - and this was an important one for Amalia – lose their shape, leaving only the memory of sensations, of emotions, as an essence of previous experiences.

♣♣♣

She finished sewing the doll's neck. It still looked good, Amalia thought to herself. Neli picked it up carefully, afraid it might break again.

— Go bye-bye!!

— Now I know she'll be in good hands! Amalia smiled at the little girl.

— You really know how to charm these little ones! said Mrs Grosu. You must have been a very good mum!

— Yes... Weren't you?

Mrs Grosu's comment managed to upset her. 'A mother's a mother till she dies!' Amalia would have shouted, but she hardly restrained herself, waiting impatiently for her neighbour to leave. A word, a phrase, an innocent remark sometimes managed to twist her, to throw reality in her face, awakening the monsters of her soul. What's the point of living in the reality that those around you clamour if it makes you suffer, if it turns you into an unearthly creature?

The ringing made Amalia shudder.

— Oh, it's probably Nelu, don't be afraid, Mrs Grosu reassured her.

Indeed, it was Nelu, carrying parcels of sweets and juice. His arrival was timely, as the children had interrupted their play and were beginning to worry about their mother's long absence.

— How kind of you. Look, my darlings, what goodies Mr Nelu has brought you! Amalia tempted them.

After long attempts, towards evening, they managed to speak to the children's mother. She hadn't been able to charge her mobile phone. She wasn't physically very ill, but the despair of having left her children to fend for themselves had made her panic. The doctors sedated her. She couldn't stop thanking her two kind neighbours.

No-one from social welfare had turned up, and the two women wondered what the little ones would have done on their own if they hadn't been looked after. Amalia Aludean agreed with Mrs Grosu. It seemed a world stricken by madness, stupidity and carelessness that showed only its ugly and absurd side, in which the natural world was dissolving. The feeling persisted that these were only the prelude to worse events, more frightening than the pandemic itself, something undecipherable but threatening. But maybe it was just the fear that lurked in every man's soul, who knew?

— Tomorrow morning, their father would come for them. Today, you know, he didn't have much chance. He was too drunk. Oh. I hope they're not giving you too much trouble and they're being good.

— Very well behaved!" nodded Amalia Aludean, nodded in agreement by Mrs Grosu.

— Mummy, Auntie Aludean gave me a doll. Her name's Lili.

— Did you thank her?

— Er... the little girl put her thumb in her mouth as she always did when she felt insecure, looking ashamedly at the screen of her mobile phone.

Mummy smiled at them, advised them to be more obedient and encouraged them, telling the children that she would see them soon.

Before retiring with her boyfriend, Mrs Grosu gave the children a bath and got them ready for bed. She asked Amalia.

— I'll come in the morning to help you with breakfast. If there's any trouble, ring the doorbell, I'll be there, no matter what time.

They said good night. Amalia watched the two leave for the flat opposite as she closed the door. Their small, seemingly insignificant gestures, such as a handshake, spoke of a special sentimental relationship.

— Go to bed. In the morning, your father will pick you up.

The little girl seemed excited, but the little boy's face looked rather sad.

— Won't you tell us a story?

— A story? Amalia realised she didn't know the stories. Maybe you can tell me one, she suggested.

— Yes! Once upon a time there was an old man and an old woman... began the little girl. She was older than your grandmother... And they had no children. But they wanted a child. As the old woman went into the forest, she saw a little girl standing by the side of the path, and she picked her up and took her to her. But the little girl grew big. But I forgot to say she was very beautiful. And they took her to the palace. There, the Emperor himself recognised her. She was his daughter, because no one else in the country was as beautiful... Are you paying attention?

— Yes, sure, sure...

— And the emperor gave a ball. But Prince Charming came to the ball from across the seas and lands. And asked the Emperor for the girl's hand in marriage. In the end, if he saw that the girl liked him... he gave her to him. And he went far, far away... And they had a big, big, fairy-tale wedding. And she had a long, long, white dress...

The little girl yawns.

— Oh, God, you've got the stories all mixed up again, Dănuț warned her, but the little sister didn't answer. She had fallen asleep with her finger in her little mouth and an unspoken word on her lips.

Chapter 9

Another story burst from Amalia's memories. It was old, but it seemed so vivid, as if it was yesterday...

Dorian had dispelled her fears, overcome her shyness. He had shown her a face unknown to others. She liked to talk about serious things, and not infrequently, they conversed about the authors and poems they had discovered and which, after a period of severe Bolshevik oppression, had sprung up as soon as they had the opportunity, with all the tight and unbridled vigour of the years of Soviet occupation. Amalia could swear that he enjoyed their conversations in the same way.

The magic of poetry often kept them company, for he often recited love verses by Blaga or Labiș, and they had discovered Nichita Stănescu together. With the help of Dorian, who was much more up-to-date with new trends in music, she discovered rock. For his own sake, he also endeavoured to listen to modern music, realising that he was beginning to like it. They went to the theatre and often lingered over a beer or a glass of wine on the terrace. Amalia savoured the bohemian life of the capital for the first time, realising the power of youth to turn the impossible into the possible. And for the first time, she felt good about herself. She was always radiant, confident, marvelling at the speed and depth of this transformation. Love - this was the very miracle!

One evening, coming out of a concert, Dorian pulled out a ring inlaid with an amber amethyst. He twirled it thoughtfully between his fingers, took Amalia's hand and put it on the ring finger of his left hand.

- You deserve a gold engagement ring, not silver and a precious stone. Precious, like you... But... the times, the possibilities..., you know how it is...

— It's marvellous, Dorian! Most beautiful!

Amalia's eyes sparkled with delight.

She looked at her ring in disbelief. The light from a lantern created playful golden ripples deep in the stone. She felt flooded with hope, and if anyone had asked her what colour hope was, she would have answered on the spot: golden, like the amber on her finger!

– I'm glad you like it so much! he said, delighted by her reaction. I would have wanted something else for you as an engagement ring...

– Are you asking me to be your fiancée? Amalia wondered. Dorian laughed. I don't even know what to put. You took me by surprise!

– Look, Amalia, you're the kind of girl any man in his right judgement would want to marry. Besides, it's more practical to get married before you get your assignment. And then it's time to settle down, hang up the fun and follies. I, myself, can't complain, I've known enough.... I'm not sorry, but once I'm out of college, I've got to think seriously. I'm going to be posted as an engineer who knows where and I'd hate to go on my own... I'd love to have someone like you on my side. I feel like I could build a home with you. Would you follow me, wherever that may be? And then come back to Bucharest, of course, as we both wish...

– Oh! I love you! I love you! I love you!

Amalia leapt into his arms, chaining his neck, kissing him with the force of a long-suppressed passion. They stopped wondering. Their footsteps seemed to take the initiative, leading them towards the Regie, towards the student dormitories. Fate had favoured them, first because they had managed to outwit the vigilance of the dormitory guard, and then because it was Saturday and Dorian's classmates were away in the country. With all her passion stripped bare, with all her confidence in a future with the most coveted young man in her university, Amalia gave herself to him, finally knowing the miracle of love fulfilled. She had discovered the mystery of life. She had become a woman. The morning window was opening, bringing the promise of a sunny day, just as Amalia's soul was opening to a future that came with the promise of happiness.

Dorian walked her home. He wrapped his arm around her shoulders protectively.

– I can manage. I'm of age, she smiled happily.

– I should come and meet your parents one day, when you say so, to let them know that I'm courting you, that I do have serious intentions. Then let's go to my parents, so they can meet you too, and let everyone know of our plans. How's that?

Amalia felt like she was floating. It seemed unreal, but she was already making plans in her amorous mind. They kissed each other eagerly, not caring if anyone could see them.

Later, in the quiet of the room, she fingered her ring, twirled the ring she'd received. For her, it was the most precious ring possible, a symbol of their love. She rewound the thread of events, reliving everything that had happened between them with the greatest intensity.

'God, I never knew it could be so beautiful.' she thought to herself.

She couldn't wait to introduce Dorian to his parents. She could have sworn they would be thrilled with her boyfriend. Student, intelligent, kind and handsome - what more could she want? As for his material situation, who cared in those days? Anyway, she guessed he wasn't doing badly, as Dorian's father was the mayor of the local community. But who really cared?

But she hadn't expected her mother to be so circumspect, even fiercely against him. Although she had been polite and invited him to the table, Mrs. Cornelia Aludean was very reserved, speaking little, biting her lips from time to time, a sign of great restraint of words that were meant to be spoken and imprecations that were meant to be kept silent. Her father countered her mother's coldness with good humour and banter, a revealing sign to everyone that he had seized the occasion and served more drinks than his wife would have liked. As for Malvina, she was studying Dorian without shyness, with the air of seeing an extra in their house.

— "You know, I have serious intentions with Amalia," Dorian ventured, overcoming his reluctance. I ask your permission to let her come with me to the country, to Vultureni, where I'm from, so that she can meet my parents. Perhaps next Saturday...

— Do I know? my mum takes over the conversation. Maybe you need more time before that, to get to know each other better...

— I think it's the right thing to do, insisted Dorian.

— Of course, it's the right thing to do! intervened with the father. That's common sense.

— Perhaps it's too early, Cornelia Aludean raised her voice. Anyway, I will agree, but on one condition: that Malvina goes with them. This will only be possible on 1 May when she's free from school. There's no way Amalia can go on her own, being unmarried.

— Hurray! Malvina claped.

— You shut your mouth! her mum urged her angrily.

Amalia had broken the oppressive silence that had fallen after Dorian's departure.

— I don't understand what you have against him, Mummy!

— It's not for you, child!

— All your life, you've been trying to show me that I'm ugly and stupid, that I don't deserve better from fate! Even now, you can't bear to know me happy? What have I done to make you hate me so?

— Have you gone mad? Has love gone mad? How can you

talk to me like that? How can you say I hate you? Have you no shame? Well, well, I reckon you deserve better than that. This boy's no good for you. Can't you see his eyes don't fit his head? He'll ruin your life! Gosh! I have such a bad feeling! But I can't choose for you who to fall in love with... You've disappointed me, Amalia, my mother added, I thought you were more mature, I thought you were smarter, and her sigh was so sincere and strong that Amalia shuddered.

She retreated into the room, crying. It's hard to please her as if you didn't know! Malvina tried to calm her down.

— Isn't he clever, Malvina?

— Yes, and he's a student, he's not the village tractor driver. He's going to be an engineer!

— Yes, he was. Very polite. He was even polite to me. He asked me what college I wanted to go to, what films I liked...

— Isn't it beautiful? Amalia interrupted her.

— Woaw... He looks like that French actor..., I can't remember his name...

— So? What can she have against him?

— Leave mum alone! Do what your heart tells you. No one lives your life but you. Listen to your little sister: you're the only one who counts, and if you feel that something makes you happy, go ahead with your head held high, without caring what that person says... or that... But do you hear? whispered Malvina after a short pause. Is he as good in bed?

Malvina's giggling is still stirring Amalia's worries.

— 'You're bringing everything into the mess, Malvina! Amalia apostrophises her without much conviction.

— Come on, tell me, tell me! insists Malvina, clapping her hands.

Amalia let herself be shrouded in the memory of those

moments. She let the silence settle in for a while, then exclaimed:

– Wonderful! Sublime!

The conversation with her sister was good for her, it was imbued with her optimism and goodwill, something she could never remember ever having experienced. She fell asleep with the thought of Dorian and the burning desire to escape from that house where she had been neither loved nor appreciated...

Chapter 10

She liked Ana and Marin Doineanu, Dorian's parents, and had every sign that the feeling was mutual. As Amalia had been introduced as their son's fiancée, they quickly advanced wedding talks. 'We're practical people,' Mr Doineanu explained. In the evening, on the porch, they sat and talked, making plans.

– I'd say let's have the wedding here in the country. We've been to many weddings here and you won't come out in the losses, Dorian's father said. What does she care about where the wedding is? Amalia thought only that she would share her whole life with him. That was enough.

– Well, he'll have it our way, Marin Doineanu intervened. It's May... If we keep it till autumn, we'll have enough time to get ready. What do you say, my son, is autumn good after the harvest?

– Won't it be too cold in October? Dorian wondered.

Sensing a certain haste in the man who was to become her husband, Amalia rejoiced, feeling grateful to Heaven that she had brought him into her life.

– Maybe, but after we harvest the vines, we'll have wine. The plums ripen by then and we'll make brandy. We're better off. And we'll either have the wedding here, in our house, or at the Cultural Centre. We recently renovated the old boyars' stables. They look great now! We hold balls here at least once a month.

– Well, yes, complete Ana Doineanu. There would be drinks, but there would also be food, because it's customary for everyone to bring something: a chicken, a piece of meat, sausages... Everyone brings what they can. The women in the village make sausages and soup. Yes, weddings are beautiful here. And we'll do our best, we have a boy!

– And there are some very good barmen. They're called in for baptisms, weddings and funerals. You'll have a chance to see them on Saturday night, it's the ball. Girls and boys come from many villages to have fun and party. Many young people make wedding preparations after the Vultureni ball! And Ducu got married last week. We were there.

— Well, when I was young, weddings lasted three days, Ana Doineanu emphasises. Hey, many men have pricked their fingers to save their honour! laughed Dorian's father.

Amalia was impressed by the Doineanu family's efficiency. She liked the way they complemented each other. Dorian watched them, too, with pride.

— You'll meet the godparents at the ball on Saturday," says Dorian's father. They're from the neighbouring village, but I've sent word for them to come. Their parents met us and baptised Dorian. We'll talk to them, let them tell us how much they'll give you and see what gifts we'll give them.

— 'Here, get up, let me see you,' the future mother-in-law said to Amelia.

Amalia complied, somewhat surprised by her request. She already considered her a mother-in-law and was convinced that it would not be difficult for her to call her mother in the future. It seemed obvious that she liked this woman.

— I was thinner than you when I married and smaller...

— Oh, you were skin and bones. You were so skinny.

— But I saw what there was to see! Look, what a beautiful woman she's grown! A super-sexy woman!

The woman blushed with delight. The warm relationship between Dorian's parents gave Amalia a sense of wellbeing and trust. After all, he was their child, raised in such a family atmosphere. She imagined that Dorian would be the same.

—Come on, let's see the wedding dress. There's plenty of material on the sides, it can be made bigger and shorter.

The two women went to the 'new house' at the back of the courtyard. Dorian's mum pulled out a long white lace dress from a chest that had been kept in excellent condition despite the passing of time.

Here, put it next to you and see how it fits! Dorian's mother invites her.

Amalia gladly complied. She was curious, too.

– Ooh! But you look lovely. Come and see for yourself.

He took her into the hallway, where there was a big mirror. Amalia couldn't believe it. Her heart was pounding with joy. She pulled her hair back in a bun. She thought she suddenly became beautiful.

– It's, it's, it's... it's beautiful! I'll adjust her waist and shorten it. She hugged Mrs. Doineanu warmly. It had been a spontaneous gesture, but so unusual for Amalia that as soon as she made it, she stopped, ashamed.

– I'm glad you like it! Look, my girl, how the tradition goes on!

Amalia also liked the nickname "my girl."

After they went to bed in the girls' yurt, Amalia, feeling cozy inside, fell asleep immediately, unlike Malvina, who was tossing and turning, seeming to be completely out of place.

Vultureni had that magical natural scenery. Located in the sub-Carpathian area of the Vâlcea region, it was surrounded by hills. On the highest, farther away, there were deciduous forests. Amalia imagined how beautiful it would be there in October, when the autumn leaves would display their varied colors, delighting the eye. Closer to the village, on the lower hills, the vineyards stretched out like blankets on the hillsides. From the top of one of the hills, you could see a silvery wisp - it looked that way from that distance. It was the river Olt, coming to maturity among the whites, flowing quietly, carrying in its waves the shadows of the past, the history of the place.

In the evenings, the peasants gathered in front of the gates, on the white mats, waiting for passers-by. It was the way news spread through the village, everyone knowing what everyone was doing, telling stories. That hadn't changed. The only thing that had changed was that no one discussed politics like before the communists came. They didn't have what or how.

– I love it here in the country! Malvina giggled, bouncing in the doorway.

Her sister's words took Amalia by surprise. She couldn't believe that Malvina, who was easily bored and was always looking for something to arouse her interest, who was seemingly cut out for the urban world, would appreciate this stay in the country.

– I didn't expect that! replied Amalia. Do you really don't mind those chickens roaming around the yard? Or the fact that you have to wash yourself in that makeshift shower in the garden with cold water?

– Ha, ha! That's the charm.

– To tell you the truth, I'd prefer to be able to wash in the tub, Amalia replied. It's a pain to wash your dishes and pots without running water. Not to mention washing clothes and carpets. We haven't had any rain, but these unpaved streets must get muddy when it rains. But I'm most horrified by flies. You just can't get rid of them.

– Well, well! You're a born princess! Try to see what's beautiful. The scenery, the silence of the night. You feel that you're dissolving in the silence, that you're sinking into this big universe as if you were a little star...

– What do you know? I had no idea I had such a romantic sister.

— Anyway, you won't have to stay here. You'll work in a city somewhere and live in a block. You'll just come here to visit. So you can enjoy the charms of village life, huh?

— I expected you wouldn't like the hustle and bustle here, knowing how you love the hubbub of Bucharest!

— The first night, I didn't sleep a wink. As if I was missing something! But now I sleep sound asleep. How can I not sleep when I wake up so quickly? These roosters have a different biorhythm than us, they sing like crazy at four in the morning, but I like it. The most beautiful is the sunset, have you noticed? It's like the whole sky's on fire.

— Well, we're on fire with all the heat during the day. It's the hottest First of May I can remember!

— You can cool off in the garden shower... A mischievous smile lit up Malvina's face. And at night, you can see the stars twinkling. I imagine them whispering.

— Yep, your mind is rattling in your head, Amalia apostrophizes her.

— You're so like mom! You are senseless, my sister! Let's get ready for the ball. I can hardly wait!

— Do you expect soft music? Oh, no, no. It'll be popular music, and you won't like it...

— Yes, but I hear there'll be a lot of boys there! Malvina whispers.

Amalia blushed. Although she had put on a thin layer of lipstick, she thought it was too bright. She dared to put a dab of lipstick on her cheeks. She would have asked Malvina, more experienced with blush, to help her, but she was already in the courtyard. She took Malvina's pencil and, with trembling hands, drew a line over her eyelashes, just as she had seen her do.

Dorian and Malvina were waiting for her.

– Ha, ha! Malvina laughed infectiously, contaminating Dorian as well.

She shouldn't have tried to outline her eyes with black, nor should she have put red on her cheeks, Amalia told herself. She was red enough now. And insecure again. She tried to get past Malvina's comment but couldn't, so all the way to the Cultural Center, she was silent while Malvina, bubbly, recounted the verbiage of a lot of nonsense. All the joy in the world seemed to have gathered on her face. Amalia was convinced that if she tried to open her mouth, all the anger that her sister's comment had stirred up would boil over. Malvina was looking very good, full of energy and cheerfulness. At the Cultural Center, the fun had already started.

Young people were holding their arms behind their shoulders and dancing a fierce traditional Romanian dance. Their steps bounced on the floor to the music. Many of their parents had come, partly because they had learned that the mayor himself was present and that his handsome son was going to introduce his future fiancée, and partly to keep an eye on their offspring, anticipating possible relationships. The gossip quickly took wings and flew around the village, quelling the curiosity of those who, for various reasons, were not present.

Amalia spotted Dorian's parents and waved to them.

– Let me introduce Florică, our godfather, and Lina, his wife," said Dorian.

The girls introduced the two. They seemed friendly to Amalia, and this made her switch her mind from her annoyance.

– You see, Silica, my sister, must be here somewhere, you should meet her too, Dorian's mother said to Amalia.

– Oh, I'd love to dance! Malvina said suddenly.

– What's the problem? Join in the dance, urged Ana Doineanu.

– Well, I don't know the steps, I've never danced to popular music. Won't you show me? Pleaseeeee, she tempted Dorian with a languorous look.

– All right, come on, I'll take you dancing. Watch my steps and follow me, followed Dorian.

Malvina and Dorian entered the horde. Only after a few small hesitations, Malvina quickly caught her stride and roared heartily, her chestnut brown hair bouncing on her shoulders. Her breasts jiggled up and down in tune with the music, attracting bolder glances.

Dorian's mother wandered off a little to exchange a word with a cousin, assuring Amalia that she would be back soon, while Marin Doineanu was happy to leave and have a glass of wine with the villagers. A pretty young woman approaches Amalia and, after a period of silence, enters into a conversation with her.

– Dorian is getting married! I can hardly believe it! He wasn't the type to rush to settle down. But when your magic comes for you, there's no escape. Dorian's fiancée is gorgeous! You can see that mutual spark between them... Gosh! I haven't introduced myself. I'm Dorina. I have been Dorian's mate since high school.

Amalia senses from the nostalgic tone in Dorina's voice that there was more to it, but she doesn't feel any resentment towards the girl. Instead, the remark about Dorian's "fiancée" clouded her mind. He watched the two of them dancing happily. The involuntary touches of their bodies as they danced seemed guilty.

– I saw you walk in with them. Are you related to the bride-to-be? Dorina asked.

–I am the bride herself! replied Amalia, a little more stiffly.

It was Dorina's turn to change.

– I'm terribly sorry, but I didn't know! God, what a blunder! Dorina put her hands to her mouth as if she could no longer stop the words already spoken. Please believe me, I didn't mean it!

Dorian's mother returned to Amalia's side. Noticing Dorina's embarrassment, she took Amalia by the hand.

– Come, my dear, meet my sister, Silica.

As she answered Silica kindly, Amalia, glancing from time to time towards the dancing area, told herself, not without a frown, that she must stay and keep these women company while Malvina and Dorian were having fun.

The two had come back from the dance in high spirits. Malvina already had damp strands of sweat clinging to her forehead, and her blouse clung to her body, instantly showing off her curves.

– Let me catch my breath and then we'll go dancing, Dorian addressed Amalia.

They were dancing, indeed. What's more, the musicians changed the register and sang Zaraza with deep feeling.

She had nothing more to reproach her future groom's behavior that evening, in the hours that followed, nor the next day when the three of them went for a walk together in the hills of the village. She blamed herself for the feeling of absurd jealousy that was creeping around him, but, after all, that's jealousy - irrational.

A childhood friend of Dorian's whom they had met in the alley had taken a picture of them, immortalizing the moment and their hopeful youth.

They had all arranged the final details of the wedding, so that by the time they left, all the plans had been made down to the last detail.

On the way back, only Amalia was awake. Next to her, Dorian looked as if he had dozed off as soon as they had left the station, and in the front seat, Malvina was asleep, too.

The green hills lagged behind. The plains showed the bright yellow expanse of the rapeseed crop, in patches of which were visible corn poppies.

Amalia had a strange feeling that a shadow had been slipping between her and Dorian ever since that evening at the Cultural Center. She couldn't understand why she couldn't get rid of that unpleasant feeling. She repeated to herself that it was only in her head that all sorts of imaginings were going on, and she reproached herself that, having every reason to be happy, she was unable to fill herself completely with this state, to live it, to consume it as it was offered to her.

"Allow yourself!" he repeated to himself. He looked at Malvina. She seemed happy even when she was asleep. "How could she be happy?"

The answer promptly popped into her mind - "Malvina always had everything she wanted" - and was immediately followed by another - "And she always got rid of what she wanted to get rid of."

Chapter 11

Amalia watched her neighbor's two little children upstairs, Neli and Dănuț, sleeping peacefully. They will have a lifetime ahead of them. Every existence has its more or less happy story. But no one could foresee the end... Looking at it from this perspective, Amalia felt it was important to love the present, to cherish every moment. After all, it's the only thing you can be sure of. You can't relive it, you can't change it, and you never know what tomorrow will bring... Except that she, Amalia, had managed to do that too few times and, ironically, each time, that state of joy of living was followed by disaster.

She envied Malvina that she had managed to enjoy life exactly the way she wanted! She did not watch from the sidelines, but walked the path of life right through the middle of it.

The little girl's rustle and a quick movement of her feet drew Amalia's attention in her direction. But Neli was asleep, probably dreaming. The smile on the child's lips assured her that it was a sweet dream.

Except that a beautiful dream can also turn into a nightmare, Amalia thought, still observing Neli, smiling after her dream.

She prayed that her neighbor would get better soon and not develop a serious form of COVID infection. What would these little ones do if left without a mother and with an irresponsible father? How selfish men can be, sacrificing anyone, even their own children, for the sake of pleasure! Their father didn't come to pick them up because he was too drunk! He was just one of many men who did this, Amalia concludes.

In her analysis, of course, she omitted those cases she knew of, where men were the pillars of their families. She generalized her own experience, more or less consciously.

Amalia woke up in the morning tired after a shallow sleep,

interrupted by repeated awakenings. She had large bags under her eyes and the look of an exhausted man. Neli and Dănuț, on the other hand, with their energies restored, were bustling about the room, running after each other.

The doorbell rang. Amalia looked through the peephole but saw nothing. The corridor, devoid of any windows, was as dark in the daytime as it would be at night unless the lights were on. She stepped back. Again the doorbell rang, more insistent this time.

– Answer, answer, the children called altogether.

Maybe it's father.

Amalia looked through the peephole again. Darkness. Not a man in sight. Who knows who was playing practical jokes? Maybe that kid downstairs... she thought. She opened the door cautiously.

Before her - still darkness. As she decided to close it again, she heard a voice coming from somewhere upstairs. Reflexively, she looked up and saw a head, and her first impression was that it was hanging from the ceiling. She let out a terrified scream.

– Don't be frightened, lady. I'm a good man! Your former neighbor! I understand you have my children.

After her eyes adapted to the darkness, Amalia realized that a very tall, dark-skinned man was standing in front of her, wearing a black sweater. She recognized him. She felt like laughing at her blunder, but she was also annoyed that she hadn't been able to censor her reactions.

– Daddy, Daddy, the child threw herself into her arms. The little boy stood back, a little more reserved.

– Thank you for looking after them... You're a very special person.

– Oh, you don't have to thank me. I did what anyone would do.

Amalia invited the man in, served him coffee while she

gathered the children's things.

– I hope their mother gets better soon.

– So do I. You know, I can't keep them at home for long.

The man looked tired and sad, but he looked lovingly at his children. She didn't know much about the married life that her upstairs neighbors had had, but concluded that some people are unable to appreciate what life has to offer and run after illusions.

– I'm here in case you need me... And Mrs. Grosu, the neighbor, helped us...

– Daddy, when is Mommy coming? Won't you take us to Mommy?

– Mommy is fine and she'll come soon.

We'll manage together for now.

– Daddy, look, I got a doll from Auntie Aludean... Isn't she beautiful?

– Yes, great! Thanks again, he said to Amalia.

After the children and their father left, Amalia decided to sort out Malvina's belongings and give them away. On the morning news on TV, the rate of increase in SARS-Cov 2 cases was announced to be stagnating. Agatha must have been watching the news, too, so she could expect a sudden visit at any moment.

She began to gather and sort through her clothing. She packed up Malvina's dresses, pants and skirts after going through her pockets. He found only a fifty-dollar bill and two three-year-old Winter Garden Theatre tickets. They seemed the only reminders of her sister's American life. She put them on the bed, organizing them by category.

She took a box to put in it the books Malvina had bought after her arrival in the country. An inner urge led her to leaf through them carefully, page by page, as if she were looking for something in particular. She had the strange sensation that the invisible fingerprints left by her sister were turning into a touch that burned her fingers.

Her sister had also brought two books with her from the USA and a society magazine. She probably put them there to read on the plane. Who knows? She started with the magazine. It was a women's magazine with health columns, a longer article on leukemia, another on nutrition-related diseases, and many others on fashion, sex and social life. Generous pages were dedicated to Marlene Dietrich, with many photos of the artist. She was the singer who made Lili Marlene famous.

Malvina played with Amalia's mind even after death. Lili Marlene... Lili... Her little girl! Marlene... Their daughter!

She stared blankly for a while. He drew a deep breath and took the books. Between the pages, she found several color photographs. In one, seemingly older, he discovered a beautiful, slender, brown-haired, blue-eyed young woman smiling mysteriously.

"Lili! It's Lili!" Amalia heard a voice out of nowhere.

"It's not Lili! It's not Lili! cried another inner voice! It's Marlene! It's Marlene, Malvina's daughter! Ha, ha! And Dorian's!"

"It's Lili!"

"No, it isn't! Can't you see she has a bigger mouth and a straighter nose? It's Marlene!" shouted the second voice.

Amalia was convulsed by a commotion, the words echoing, overlapping one another...

She clutched her head in her hands, covering her eyes.

– Shut up! Stop it! Amalia screamed.

Then she lay limp and dizzy in the chair beside her, her head in her hands. It hurt her terribly.

At a certain point, the voices ceased, and a dead silence fell over the room. A chill ran through her from head to foot, making her tremble as if she were being drained. She had felt something similar when her mother told her that Malvina had given birth to a little girl she had named Marlene. Dorian had become a father—this time to a wanted child. The hatred for them, for their child, erupted volcanically with every heartbeat.

Amalia struggled to her feet, turned on the television, searching for an entertainment channel. One of them was a folk dance troupe. Young men and women dressed in flowered folk shirts were playing in a popular dance. On the left side of the screen was the name of the dance group. He had never heard of it, but seeing it reminded him of another dance band and other painful events...

Chapter 12

Young Amalia was aware that lately, she was the one looking for Dorian. She would call him at the dormitory and often there was no answer or the doorman would inform her that the student Doineanu was not available, and when she managed to talk to him, Dorian was motivated that he had to study. Amalia would go to the dorm on her own initiative to meet him, to talk, "to keep him company, to encourage him." He became more and more grumpy and, on a few occasions, snapped at her. The girl tried to be as reasonable as possible, not to talk back. She was afraid. She feared lest he might find some reason to break it off, even though she knew that things were moving towards marriage, that the wedding was already fixed. She avoided inviting him home because her mother didn't like him and Malvina seemed to like him too much. He wasn't lying when he said he had to learn. So did she. After all, their last exam session was just around the corner and they had to take their license. Sometimes Amalia managed to sneak into Dorian's room in the dormitory, especially on weekends, when his roommates were away in the provinces. Then, it was the two of them studying together. From time to time, they also made love, but Amalia pretended not to notice that this happened more at her insistence. She remarked that Dorian still made time to go to folk dances at least three times a week, a fact that surprised her, knowing that he was rather fond of rock and rock'n roll, of that modern music she still didn't really understand, but which she made an effort to listen to for her fiancé's sake. Then she saw him at the ball, dancing in a popular dance, and he seemed, it's true, like a country boy who had grown up with rural traditions, perfectly integrated into the place... It struck her that she could learn to dance folk music. After all, why not? Dorian seemed to like it and they were going to have a country wedding...

Dorian, will you take me to... Alunelu (name of a Romanian folk dance)?

I'd really like to learn folk dancing.

– No, Amalia. Only the selected ones go to the Alunelul, the best, because they do tours, shows.

The creases between his eyebrows warned that this was a subject on which she no longer wished to comment.

– Oh, then, at least let me watch... I think it's very nice! Amalia insisted, despite the fact that she had noticed her discontent.

– They warned us not to bring anyone from outside the troupe so as not to distract the dancers. Everyone is stressed about the tour and the competition. We need to get ahead of the „Călușari" (famous Romanian folk dance). No one goes there accompanied, Amalia.

Amalia accepted the explanation, blaming herself for her lack of understanding. Besides, even if she wanted to comment, she couldn't. She felt that if she opened her mouth, she would vomit. It wasn't the first time she'd been suddenly nauseous, and the lateness of her period suggested why.

When she was sure she was pregnant, she was elated and often smiled for no reason. She became dreamy, making plans for the future, imagining what she would do if it was a boy or a girl, what name would suit them.

"I'm going to be the best mom ever!" she told herself. A feeling of love suddenly struck her. It was just like when she had held the doll she had longed for in her arms as a child, only this time it wasn't a doll, but something real: her child, their child.

She was reluctant to confess all this to Dorian, planning to surprise him on his birthday. She had booked a seat at the restaurant, having gotten the money for it from her father without her mother's knowledge.

It wasn't the fanciest restaurant, but it didn't matter. The event itself was going to be memorable. They ordered marrow and a white wine to match.

– Dorian, I have a birthday present for you.

– Other than inviting me to the restaurant? Dorian smiled. The wine had made him a little more cheerful and optimistic.

Amalia smiled in her turn, took a deep breath and looked at Dorian with eyes filled with tears of happiness.

– I'm pregnant! We're going to have a baby, do you realize? Amalia radiated happiness and joy at sharing the miraculous news.

She saw the change in her lover's face. He was shocked. She told herself it was only natural. He was going to be a father! Hadn't she been just as startled at first?

After a time of oppressive silence, Dorian grimaced with disgust, picked up the napkin from the table and threw it in Amalia's face.

– You're having an abortion, Amalia! You will not be an obstacle for my future!

– But what's the point? We're getting married anyway.

– That's just it, darling. I was going to tell you, but I postponed it till after the study session. We're not getting married. You're not going to thrust marriage on me so young. Do you understand?

– But... not long ago we arranged the wedding at Vultureni, Amalia.

– We're not getting married, period. If you don't want to have a bastard, have an abortion. I know a woman, a former midwife. She's good. She got me out of trouble once. Let me write down your address.

Dorian reached into his purse for a pen, grabbed a piece of napkin from the table and hastily wrote down the address.

– What did I do wrong?

He was silent. He was looking in his wallet for something.

A few curious onlookers at neighbouring tables stared at them. Amalia felt the whole restaurant spinning with her and those eyes were spinning too. She felt a strong nausea and a pang in her stomach.

–Take this money for the abortion, she heard Dorian through the fog. You pay for the meal... And Amalia, don't come looking for me! Ever! He left her alone at the table, staring into space. Unable to utter a word or move, she looked like a statue.

She didn't know how she got home, and in the days immediately following, she could remember almost nothing, only the echo of voices she couldn't understand, floating in a thick fog.

That period after the brutal separation from Dorian had largely faded from her mind. Only a few glimpses of memories had survived the test of time, the one where she'd run madly through the streets, sometimes running to exhaustion, without any particular purpose, coming home only to sleep, or the one where she'd thrown the ring she'd received from Dorian into an old trunk, never wanting to see it again. Far from feeling liberated by this gesture, she believed that all her feelings had suddenly grown old, that they were left behind, trapped, unable to return, like the fossilized past, encased in that amber-yellow stone.

She felt no hatred then, no love, no forgiveness, detached from everything that surrounded her as if she were at a great distance from everyone and everything, in a weightlessness of spirit. It simply didn't feel anything - a robot programmed only to eat and walk. With her thoughts wandering, she was incapable of reason, of making decisions, of acting. She almost forgot to speak, avoiding conversation.

She had also failed to show up for college, forgoing her

degree exam.

Whether or not those around her were concerned about her condition, if they were worried, she couldn't remember.

This nightmare disappeared after a month and was replaced by an even bigger one. A scream from the kitchen, followed by crying.

— No! [Screams] Oh, my God! The mother's despair chilled Amalia, but it also had the power to bring her out of the emotional wilderness she had entered.

Her mother sat with a letter in her hand, wet with tears, while her father tried unsuccessfully to console his wife. The scene seemed strange to Amalia, as she couldn't remember ever seeing her mother cry. She had always given her the impression of a strong person, for whom there was no insurmountable obstacle in life, able to control everything... An unfelt dread was taking shape in the girl's soul.

— You're to blame, Amalia, her mother said, the moment she saw her standing in the doorway. You brought that monster into my house...

— What's the matter? Amalia didn't know if she had really managed to utter the question or if she was only miming.

— Malvina ran away with Dorian! My child! My little girl, my darling, is gone and I don't know if I'll ever see her again!

Mrs. Cornelia Aludean was sobbing.

The shock prevented Amalia from saying another word. She hadn't known about the relationship between the two, but she had sensed it, refusing to give the idea a clear outline.

— It'll be all right, Cornelia! You'll see. And you'll see her too. Their father seemed much calmer in the situation.

— How can I see her if she's fled the country? Who knows where she is now and what will become of her!

– At least she had the courage to do it. We stay here and put up with communism. You should be happy for her. She'll live free, in a free country, you shouldn't pity her.

– Shut up, or someone will hear us! The Security will come to investigate about it anyway.

Her mother went out of the kitchen to pour out her tears and suffering in the solitude of her room.

– Your sister and the one you brought into our house went on tour with the "Alunelul" dance troupe. They lost their trail in Belgium, apparently. They ran away. But your mom found this letter hidden in the file drawer. Malvina knew we wouldn't be looking there so soon!

Amalia remained silent while her father, usually so taciturn, now spilled everything he had learned.

"That's why he didn't want me to go to the dances! All this time, they were meeting there!" Amalia felt like she was suffocating. She remembered their last night together at the restaurant.

"The baby! I'm pregnant!" The reality hit her like a thunderbolt. Too consumed with her suffering, she had stopped thinking about the baby. She hadn't really thought about anything after that grim parting. As if someone had suddenly fueled her hatred, her hatred took off, gaining energy - an evil energy.

She dug in the pocket of the dress she had worn on her last meeting with Dorian and found the napkin with the midwife's name and address written on it.

Chapter 13

She named her Lili, after her former doll. The little girl had stubbornly insisted on being born despite her mother's best efforts to get rid of her. The decree banning abortions had been passed, so she turned to a retired midwife who, for a few hundred lei, helped women to miscarry unwanted pregnancies. Clandestinely, of course. She rented a small, dilapidated house in a slum on the outskirts of the capital, moving her makeshift "practice" often so as not to be discovered if any of the women were more outspoken and revealed the illegality.

Amalia was unlucky. The workmanship had produced a massive hemorrhage that so frightened the midwife on occasion that she dragged Amalia out of the room and left her in the middle of the night on the street, bleeding, in terrible pain.

– Don't be frightened. I'll call an ambulance!

Don't panic. How could she when the old woman herself looked absolutely terrified!

– Don't give my name, you hear? I'm not the only one who can fuck it up, it's you too, warned the woman.

Keep her name out of it? She didn't even know his name! She only knew his first name, but she wouldn't bet on that being real, either.

Amalia was convinced she was going to die. At 23! She hadn't even reached a quarter of a century! She didn't know why the idea seemed so relevant.

Who would have thought? So young! And so? Is that the end of it? she wondered. An idea flashed through her mind: would he feel remorse? The thought quickly faded, replaced by a warm feeling. She felt the pavement with her hand. It was damp, though not raining. She slowly raised her arm and looked at him. Her palms were red. Blood. It stank. It smelled like death...

She heard the siren, a few voices, then he only saw something white, blurry, voices she couldn't tell if they were real or imaginary, and she lost consciousness.

When she woke up, she was already in a hospital ward. Her mother was standing near the door. She did not approach. Amalia looked at her, trying to anticipate her reproaches, but Mrs. Cornelia Aludean stood frozen, not saying a word. Amalia thought that she would have scolded her, she would have said something... anything. But this silence and lack of expression on her mother's face was the hardest thing she could bear.

The doctor came in. He had a cold, grim face. He invited her mother outside.

— Are you in pain? the doctor asked.

— Yes, big ones, she replied despite not noticing any compassion in his tone of voice.

— I managed to stop the bleeding... but the pains are going to linger for a while. Where there's pleasure, there's pain!

— And the child? she struggles to pronounce the word.

— She's all right.

— What?

— I managed to save her, Miss,' he emphasizes the word 'Miss' ironically.

— Oh, no! Amalia put her hand to her eyes. She felt the urge to cry but found that the tears refused to come.

— Damn bitches! You're nothing but trouble! If you like to have fun, you should like to suffer the consequences.

Amalia closed her eyes. She realized that from now on everyone would consider her a pariah. The immense hatred that seemed to infiltrate every fiber of her being flooded her again. If Dorian and Malvina were there in front of her, she would find the resources to kill them. She was sure of it. "Damn you!"

– You'll have to make a statement. There's a policeman outside waiting for me to call him.

She didn't give any statement, not to protect the midwife, but because she couldn't get another word out. The doctors concluded she was in post-traumatic shock.

She sat for hours huddled in the corner of her room, listening to those mocking voices, which had reappeared and were now laughing bellicose, wildly, this time borrowing the vocal timbre of Malvina and Dorian. At times, blurry, dark images, taking the form of female silhouettes, flashed before her gaze. She couldn't see their faces clearly, but somehow, she was convinced that they were as beautiful as they were threatening, especially when they addressed her, and she recognized either her mother's accusing voice, Malvina's ironic one, or even her own voice, cold and flat.

Amalia refused food and water. A new period then followed of which she personally remembered only the large white room with lots of beds, some showers with frozen water and the unspeakable horror of being taken to another room where she was lying on a bed and electrodes were attached to her hands and feet.

Thinking back to that time in her life, Amalia now told herself that the psychiatrists had succeeded in getting her to a state of acceptance of an implacable reality, but they had never been able to erase the hatred from her memory. But she became fully aware that she had to camouflage it, and it became a preoccupation like that of an actor who has to get into the skin of his character. Only in Amalia's case, the role was to be permanent, second nature to her.

She remembered being afraid of coming home from hospital, of her parents' reaction, of her own reaction. She didn't know what to say, nor what to do, acting like a puppet coordinated by others, lacking energy also because of the tranquilizers she had been prescribed.

She went into the room, finding it completely alien, as if he had not spent 23 years of her life there.

The door suddenly slammed against the wall and her mother entered, but Amalia didn't even flinch.

– Please come down to dinner. We have important things to discuss, Amalia! The authoritative tone contradicted the "please." Your father and I made important decisions about you.

She didn't wonder why those decisions didn't include her.

– First, take your pills, and then eat, her mother ordered.

Amalia obeyed, swallowing mechanically without tasting anything.

– You'll have to leave school for a while. You'll go to Lugoj, to my mother's cousin, Auntie Nuți. You haven't had the chance to meet because our families haven't spoken. Old things. Ever since your grandfather turned your father in for being anti-communist... Yet I trust her not to divulge the secret. I've given her enough money to accept and forget our old grudges. She's in need, so she didn't have much choice. And knowing her, I know she'd be ashamed to call her niece a stupid whore...

– In Lugoj, it will be fine, you'll see, his father added consolingly. And Nuți is a good woman.

– You'll work in a laboratory as a biology assistant. After you give birth, you'll give the baby to the orphanage and forget about it. Give it up for adoption if you want to have any future. Once you're well enough, you'll come back and finish the college. See, I wasn't given that chance, Cornelia Aludean sighed.

Amalia listened passively as if it wasn't about her. She had no intention of fighting back. She didn't care. She didn't care anymore. The only thing she regretted was that she didn't die there on the cobblestones. Was she supposed to give up the baby? Perfect. After all, it was his child, Satan's child. His hatred for Dorian was also directed at the unborn child. "Damn you! Damn you all!"

The strength of the hatred she had developed for life, for society, for her parents, for Malvina and Dorian, both astonished and frightened her. As far as Malvina and Dorian were concerned, she never wanted to see or hear from them again. And this would remain a must in her life.

Chapter 14

Amalia remembered the day at the beginning of March 2020, when the first cases of COVID-19 had just been announced and Malvina had knocked on her door. She thought there was nothing in this life that surprised her anymore. And, lo and behold! After all these bitter years, her sister appeared on her doorstep, looking as if they had parted yesterday, waving a broad smile. By that smile, she recognized her immediately, and by the joy in her eyes. Those greenish-brown eyes, slightly slanted, had remained as playful as in her youth. But his vocal timbre was huskier, influenced by the number of cigarettes she smoked. It was enough to look at Malvina for her to feel a stirring of frustration, envy and hatred – a dangerous blend of emotions. In spite of her age, her sister maintained a slender body - she would later learn that she worked out every day, had a complexion free of deep wrinkles and was still beautiful. In contrast, Amalia's double chin, face that time had mercilessly carved, and white hair made her look much older than she actually was.

– Hello, won't you invite me in? Malvina asked, amused by her sister's reaction.

– Yes, sure. Come in, she replied coldly after a long moment of thought. There was astonishment and displeasure in her voice.

Malvina entered, examined the room and put down her luggage.

– Can I stay at your place until I find a place that suits me? Malvina asked. I'm back and I want to stay, she announced.

Surprised, Amalia didn't comment immediately, but went to make coffee and calm down the strong emotion of such a visit. When she returned with the cups of coffee, her lips were still pursed and she could barely control the trembling in her hand.

– Ha, ha! laughed Malvina. You look just like mom. She used to clench her lips when she didn't like something!

— You could have announced your arrival, made a phone call...

— I wanted to surprise you. I wasn't sure if I'd called, you wouldn't have left the house...

— You were as blunt as ever...

— And honest, too!

Malvina settled down, ignoring her sister's lack of enthusiasm.

— Why do you want to come back, Malvina?

— With the pension there, I can live very well here, she replied, looking out of the window. Then she turned her head, avoiding Amalia's gaze. Ah! Look! Mom's doilies. You kept them! It's like going back in time.

— It's just that we're not the same... Amalia tried so hard to rein in the anger she felt ravaging her.

- Don't tell me you've held a grudge after all these years! laughed Malvina.

Her laughter, intended to suggest surprise or disregard, sounded false. It seemed to Amalia that her sister had changed. She couldn't remember ever having heard her laugh other than willingly, from the bottom of her heart.

— Some things you can't wipe out of life, like dusting furniture, Amalia apostrophized her.

— Some things in life must simply be thrown away. It would become too cluttered not to drop some of them, and from time to time, there's a lot of cleaning up to do.

— It's great that you managed to do it. Then, may I ask why you're back in the country, and especially... here?

— Johnny's gone. I'm currently single. Well, life is life. That's it. I needed a change! Uh, Johnny? Amalia had no idea who Johnny was. She didn't think she wanted to find out. She preferred to think of her as a stranger who had crossed her threshold. Otherwise, she might strangle her.

— And you thought of coming here after all these years! Amalia exclaimed, heated.

— Well, doesn't that seem like a change? The greatest! laughed Malvina. Oh, I didn't tell you about Johnny! He was my last husband... The third, Malvina clarified, sensing her sister's puzzlement.

— Well. I see, said Amalia, but she didn't understand. She knew that she had split up with Dorian and that their daughter, Marlene, had been left in her father's care, that she had remarried, but she didn't remember calling Johnny.

— Is my mother buried here in Lugoj? Malvina changed the subject.

— Yes. And my father. At Mom's request, we brought him too, to be together.

— You did? I didn't know. She didn't tell me that. Shall we go to the cemetery tomorrow? Light a candle, bring flowers...

— I found your mom's number in your cell phone. She texted you when Dad died. I texted you when Mom died. You didn't answer. I figured it was the wrong number, you didn't get the information.

— I got it. But... I wasn't ready to come back. I preferred to carry their image as if they were alive. What could I tell them after all these years? The image of the dead always haunts you, doesn't it? You know better. Even you couldn't come to Lili's funeral!

The remark sounded reproachful. What could he have said? That it seemed improbable that Lili had died? That he'd cleaved to the illusion that Lili was still alive somewhere far away? If she had told her that, Malvina would have thought she was crazy... But wouldn't she have been right? In any case, Malvina would have been the last person to unburden herself to...

— I took care of her grave, Malvina continued, seeming not to notice her sister's confusion. Oh God! What a tragedy! She was laughing at one of my jokes, and then a madman drove the wrong way...

Malvina closed her eyes... She said nothing for a while, and then she whispered:

— I was behind the wheel. I... I pulled over as far as I could... I... I hit the guardrail... Lili...

Malvina couldn't go on. She felt like she was suffocating. Her lower lip trembled and her eyes, enlarged with horror at the memory, showed that she was reliving that terrible event.

A dead silence fell between them. A cold chill shook Amalia. For so many years she'd been trying so hard to impose the thought that Lili was still alive until she had come to truly believe it. As the ultimate evil she had done to her, Malvina had, with a word, destroyed the last stronghold she had built to survive and move on after their mother had given her the sad news, twenty-one years ago, of the girl's death. Amalia was returning to a painful, heartbreaking reality. Did Malvina realize this? Most probably not. Neither did her mother know that Amalia had found her own weapon of self-defense — a wall between the world and herself.

In their flow, the moments seemed to crackle in the intensity of the silence between the two sisters.

Malvina took out a cigarette and puffed heavily. As if the simple act of smoking gave her strength, she began to speak.

— Dorian died too, you know.

— I found out, Amalia answered dryly. Lili told me.

— Do you want to know more about him?

— No, I don't intend to.

— I guess you haven't forgiven him either! Malvina sighed.

You could do it now that he's gone! You know, I've heard that forgiveness heals souls, sets them free! I read somewhere that it brings happiness...

Amalia felt Malvina's words as a mockery, even if her face didn't express it, she looked very serious.

– Who are you, Malvina, to give me advice?

– Your sister? She smiled at her, smiling slyly, as in childhood.

Amalia avoided answering, pressing her lips together. She would have a lot to say. She would have told her that where there is no love, there is no forgiveness, and that it's too late anyway... Without Lili, everything is too late...

– I kept in touch with my mother, we talked, we phoned each other, but after my father's death, when you moved her to Lugoj, not so much... I thought maybe you wouldn't abandon her!

"It wasn't so," Amalia corrected Malvina in her mind. It got to her that you didn't dare get off your precious ass and come to Daddy's funeral, that you didn't care about her fate even when she had that damned stroke! You think she wanted me around? No, she didn't! She wanted you, her beloved daughter! But... more... Oh... most of all... she blamed you for pushing Lili to go to America to make a big career in journalism. So did I! You took my last love, Malvina! You took my baby! You took everything! My mother didn't love me, but when Lili went to America, that's when my mother knew exactly how I felt! She felt the same when you ran away from home, away from her! Then, Lili's death completely shattered her. It shook her! Understand? She really loved Lili! Maybe that's what we're given: to pass our suffering from one generation to the next. And unhappiness! You, Malvina, you've been running around looking for happiness. Have you found it? I'm afraid I haven't. But I don't really care!"

Chapter 15

He had interrupted her biology studies for medical reasons and left for Lugoj. Now, looking back, she could say she had been lucky with Nuți, her mother's relative. She had been patient with her, even if she hadn't managed to change her mood. She neither pitied nor disgusted her. She didn't blame her for anything, despite the fact that the new tenant seemed like a ghost landed in her house. Pale, silent, performing only the necessary activities. For a while Amalia paid no attention to her growing waistline, just as she was generally uninterested in the way she looked or the way she dressed. She was carrying Satan's child, and for a while, this thought obsessively repeated. She couldn't wait to get rid of it. She would do exactly as she had been told, like a puppet pulled by strings, no expectations, no regrets.

But then she felt the movement of the baby and a strange sensation that in her, a "dead" among the living, life could be born! Then, she began to live again. In its own way. Detached from everyone and everything. Nuți had gone out of her way to find her a job as a laborer at the local hospital, and the work took her out of her thoughts, mechanically executing the work she had to do. The colleagues left her alone, seeing no point in any communication other than strictly professional. She began to stop thinking of the child who had also fought for her life, despite the massive hemorrhage caused by the attempted abortion, as "Satan's child." It was her child, all hers! As the great event of the birth drew near, Amalia's thoughts began to switch from the betrayal she had suffered to the coming little one, from the past to the future, even though she was convinced that the hatred she had developed for Malvina and Dorian would never disappear, that it was like a battery that works as soon as it is charged. She preferred not to charge it, and channeled her preoccupation towards the unborn child.

Unexpectedly, the child had become a balm for her wounded soul.

— It's a girl, the nurse announced immediately after the birth. What name?

— Lili, she answered promptly.

— Liliana?

— No, just Lili.

She hadn't thought of a name. Neither boy's nor girl's. The name suddenly sprung suddenly out of a corner of her memory.

She had become a mother. The feeling came out of nowhere. When she held little Lili in her arms and watched her waving her arms and legs, when she suckled her, the feeling of belonging flooded her, the awareness that this bundle of life was a little piece of her. She looked at her with wonder and softness. She looked at her as if she was a great miracle, convinced that she was. Only Mrs. Nuți had been with her in those first weeks after the birth. She had helped her. A month later, Mrs. Cornelia Aludean came to visit them, not to see her granddaughter, but to convince Amalia to take steps to give the baby up for adoption.

— You will give the girl to the orphanage, as we agreed. I've arranged things to speed things up.

— I won't give her up.

— You have no choice, Amalia. What life do you want to give her? What life can you give her? You'll be everyone's mockery. She'll always be everyone's laughing stock, a bastard, and you'll always be the whore who created her.

— I won't give her!

— Yes you will, because you've nothing to raise her on, I'm not willing to give my hard-earned money for a bastard. Not me, nor your father! You'll give it, and you'll go back to Bucharest to finish college, to join the world. You'll repeat your last year and that's it! You'll forget what happened, believe me! As if it never happened...

You're neither the first nor the last. And you'll find an honorable guy to marry you, not a tramp like the one you're mixed up with!

— I won't give her away!

And she didn't. She realized it was the first time she had openly opposed her mother's request.

She could scream, she could beg, and she was determined not to be separated from her Lili. She didn't care about college, the world, anything. She had, for better or worse, a job and maybe, in time, she would find a better one, better paid. She went back to her room with the little girl, leaving Mrs. Aludean to Mrs. Nuți to rant all she wanted. And when Lili feigned a smile and looked at her with her clear, blue eyes, she was convinced that she would never let her out of her heart.

Nuți had supported her and for that, she was extremely grateful. She had been there for her even after Cornelia Aludean's departure, even though she no longer received the monthly allowance Amalia's parents sent her.

When Lili was three months old, her mother, this time accompanied by Mr. Aludean, again visited her.

Amalia listened stoically, until she heard Lili crying. She went to comfort her. By the time she returned with Lili to the living room where her parents were waiting, the little girl had calmed down, smiled broadly at Mrs. Aludean and stretched her tiny arms around her neck.

At that moment, Cornelia Aludean fell silent, then burst into tears to Amalia's astonishment. As surprised, she thought to herself that she had never seen her mother cry again, despite the difficult life she had led, despite her permanently unhappy air, a disturbing memory suddenly flashed back to her — her mother's heartrending cry when she had heard of Malvinas' runaway.

— I lost two girls... I don't want to lose a third... Cornelia

Aludean murmured after she calmed down. I know how you feel about me, Amalia, but at least let me be her grandmother! God, it's like someone's put a curse on us! Maybe... maybe this little girl will chase it away.... Forgive me, Amalia, if you can... forgive them all... that you may forgive yourself...

Cornelia's love for Lili faded with time, even if it did not make it disappear, Amalia's hatred towards her mother. Being even closer, integrating her and Lili into her own family, Nuți was nevertheless the one who played the role of a grandmother more during the girl's first years of life. Nuți's sudden death in her sleep affected Amalia. At that time, she had been the only person who had not only accepted her as she was, but had also taught her to accept herself for the sake of her little girl.

Chapter 16

Lili was 26 when she left, charmed by the American miracle, portrayed in such fresh and enticing colors by Malvina. She was visiting her parents for the first time since leaving the country. Amalia had refused to go to Bucharest to meet her. But Lili had settled in the capital, where she had found a job, and Malvina's arrival had become a major event in the Aludean grandparents' household, an unmissable one.

Lili had her own disappointments, dreaming of a different kind of journalism, or in her short career, she had encountered nothing but self-righteousness. The press's claim of independence was hypocrisy. Knowing her abilities, she wanted success and – why not? – even fame. Barriers in her professional life seemed to require far too much effort and time to overcome, if they could ever be overcome! Much to Amalia's exasperation, she had not found fulfillment in her love life, not seeming to be sufficiently attached to any man, seeming to be content with a few fleeting relationships, waiting to meet "what should be hers, what was put aside."

She was slightly fascinated by Malvina, always bursting with energy and vigor, by the prospect of meeting her cousin Marlene, by the "American dream" which her aunt had promised her.

– It's not easy there either, but I'm telling you, if ever there was a country where a dream could be realized, it's America!

Malvina's words sounded like a promise!

– With your intelligence, your beauty and your charm, believe me, you are going to be somebody! I can imagine you working at a famous television station.

Did she realize that when she decided to leave, she had crushed the souls of both her mother and grandmother, smashing them to pieces? No one told her at the time that she would also meet her father if she went... She learned about that later.

Amalia perceived her daughter's departure to the American continent as another evil that Malvina and Dorian were doing to her, taking away what she held dear. It was useless to talk on the phone, it was useless to tell her that she was fine and to see her feeling fulfilled and full of life, that she was happy! There was an ocean between them that stood in the way of an ordinary hug.

She didn't show her daughter how much she was suffering for fear of darkening her happiness.

Shortly after setting foot on American soil, Lili met Marlene, who had come to visit her mother to meet her cousin. Lili told her on the phone how delighted she was with Marlene.

–Mommy, if you could see her! She's beautiful! And we look alike! Like sisters, not cousins! Most people say so!

"You really are sisters," Amalia said to herself.

– You have no idea how well we get along! Maybe because we're about the same age. Pity we haven't known each other longer. You know Marlene speaks perfect Romanian?

– Yes? Good for her! Amalia added.

– She learned from her grandparents, who settled here permanently. Having only one son... you know how it is... they came too... But they died, unfortunately.

It was interesting information for Amalia. She never looked for Dorian's parents. She didn't want to hear anything about him, or anyone or anything about him. What was the use?

Amalia listened with tears in her eyes. She now understood her mother's distress at Malvina's departure. What's more, her parents had not been given the opportunity to meet their other granddaughter! Another undeserved "slap" Malvina had given them. Not even then, the one and only time she came to visit home, did she bring Marlene along!

— Marlene works for a big accounting firm. She has a very good job. What more can one want? All her dreams came true.

Amalia learns that Marlene was divorced, her marriage not being able to cope with too long and too far apart. Her ex-husband had taken a better-paying job hundreds of miles from home. And to her surprise, this seemed

to be the natural thing to do there. No one was willing to make any compromises when it came to profession and money.

— That's the way it is around here. You go where the better job pays better. You don't stay in one place for the rest of your life, like here! Anyway, I appreciate the fact that they remained friends even after they split up, even though Marlene confessed to me that she suffered a lot.

At some point, the thing Amalia had feared the most happened. It was inevitable, after all.

—I'm also going to meet Dorian, Marlena's father, Lili informed Amalia. You know, around here you don't say Mr., you just use your first name, Lili continued.

An old and long-dormant suffering was reopening... She hoped, however, not to be told that Dorian was her father. She hoped things would be left as they were. After all, no one would gain!

But she found out. She was told. Amalia suspected that Dorian had apologized, saying that when he had left, he had known that her mother was going to have an abortion, that he had not known of her existence for a long time, that Amalia and her parents were guilty of not telling anyone about the child's existence...

Lili was shocked and showed her anger towards her mother in her own way by stopping calling her, blaming her for hiding the truth.

For a while, she didn't answer her phone, filling Amalia with anxiety and despair.

When she finally did answer Amalia, it was only to accuse her.

— How could you do such a thing? It was my right to know, to know my father! And he's a great man, even if he does look a bit sullen and unhappy. But with me he was so warm, so kind... It's too bad he didn't do too well here. He didn't get a job as an engineer, but I think he'd rather not go far from home and have a schedule that allowed him to raise Marlene. Yeah! I think he sacrificed himself for his daughter! Probably, that's why he never remarried. You know what I think? That you were selfish and you never wanted to know my father! Because as far as he was concerned, he was thrilled to meet me.

Amalia felt devastated. She was experiencing that feeling of weightlessness she had once experienced after Dorian had left her. Her health was beginning to fail.

Some of Lili's indignation was also directed at her grandmother.

— Grandma, if you knew about all this, why didn't you tell me? Both you and my mother kept the truth from me! To find out after all these years that I had such a wonderful father...

Gradually, however, the love for her mother and grandmother and the longing for home overcame, and their communication began to return to normal. Even if she had not found out all the details about her parent's relationship, Lili, analysing the situation on her own, began to look at it from another perspective and wondered why Dorian had not looked for her after finding out that she had another daughter in the country and why he had gone with her mother's sister... She was unravelling some mysteries, realizing why the relationship between her mother and Malvina had been as if non-existent. She was confused. She liked Malvina a lot. She liked Dorian, too, especially since they were each in their own way trying to protect her... But she loved her mother and her grandparents...

The truth, hidden for so long, was revealed to Marlene, and she was utterly shocked, disgusted by her parents' behaviour, even refusing to speak to them. Lili, also hurt, found herself in the position of supporting her sister. Lili decided it was simpler to take things as they were, not to burden her heart with unnecessary suffering, not to judge anyone. It's easier to love than to hate someone. It also influenced Marlene to look on the bright side, that they had a chance to get to know each other.

"That's her, Amalia thought. A bright nature, preferring not to see the shadows in the character of others, unable to hold her anger against those who wronged her for long."

"Who could she be like? The Aludenians, surely not, and Dorian was an asshole..." Amalia wondered, not once. Lili's perception of her father amazed Amalia.

Has it changed so much? she wondered. Dorian, a sulky? A fleeting image of a cheerful, easy-going young man, savouring every moment of life, flashed fleetingly into his mind. Analysing what Lili had said, she concluded that he was deeply unhappy. Amalia was not sorry, after all, he deserved it. Most likely, Dorian had seen his life as a huge failure, at least, that was the conclusion Amalia had drawn from Lili's information. Some emigrants adapt easily, have accomplishments and integrate perfectly into their adopted country, as seemed to be the case with Malvinas. But for others, reality doesn't quite follow the dream. She deduced that Dorian had not found a job that matched his qualifications. On the other hand, his separation from Malvina... For her, he had left the country and for her, he had broken every principle. He really loved her! The former Don Juan of the Polytechnic had never remarried! The fact that Marlene had stayed with him didn't soften Amalia's opinion of him, on the contrary, it filled her with indignation. "She didn't want my baby, she wanted Malvina's!"

"Well, what's not to like, mother's daughter? You're the same! Hear that? Don't you ever forget that you're beautiful and smart and wonderful! You deserve the best! Amalia replied. Lili was amused by her mother's vehemence.

She didn't resent Marlene, but Amalia was deeply affected by the fact that Lili had become fond of Dorian.

Lili's news of his illness - advanced pancreatic cancer - and then of his death shortly afterwards gave Amalia a sense of peace.

"Amen. As far as he is concerned, fate has done justice in my place, although a bit too late!" concluded Amalia.

Lili was well regarded at the newspaper where she worked, opening up wonderful prospects. This made Amalia proud of her daughter, but it didn't lessen the longing and pain of knowing her so far away.

Then disaster struck... About 19 years ago, she received a phone call in the middle of the night, and Cornelia Aludean gave her the terrible news:

– Lili had died. Car... accident...

Her little girl. Her love. Her dreams. Her soul. All dead. Only hatred had survived the tragic event, gushing like lava erupting from a reactivated volcano.

After the initial shock wore off, an inner voice came out of nowhere and said, "It can't be true! Lili is alive! Far across the ocean." She clung to the echo of those words like a hanged man to his noose, preferring to place herself in another reality: her own, resenting anyone who tried to overturn her perspective.

– Are you going to the funeral? Cornelia asked her.

– Whose funeral? Who died, Mom? Amalia replied, with an absent air, as if out of nowhere.

Chapter 17

Meeting Malvina again had stirred in Amalia's soul that burning black magma. "I was driving the car." The words reverberated in her mind over and over like a succession of echoes. And it was not only the realization that it was Malvina who bore the guilt of having driven the vehicle, but also the bearer of confirmation, the voice of the witness. Malvina was undoing, without realising it, Amalia's habit of still considering her daughter alive, living across the Atlantic. For Amalia, it was as if Lili had died once more.

The peace, so arduously won, was dissolving into the darkness that enveloped her mind. The idea that she would never escape the past as long as Malvina lived crept deeper and deeper into her thoughts.

The two women preferred to avoid any discussion of their personal lives that evening, but they were well aware that it was only a postponement.

They both ate with lumps in their throats. Amalia turned on the TV. All the news channels were announcing the devastation wreaked by the enemy: the COVID-19 virus was on the attack, claiming its first victims.

For the two sisters, the news of the onset of the pandemic was an opportunity to be able to keep quiet without their silence becoming "screaming" in a way that might have seemed to anyone on the outside, the natural anxiety in the presence of such repeated breaking news.

Amalia couldn't fall asleep. She wondered why Malvina had come, why now, and couldn't find a plausible answer. She didn't believe in her "need for change," even if it was in her nature.

She finally dozed in the morning. She dreamed that she was dawdling in a haze that would occasionally roll away, letting her glimpse faces, images, various objects, and then become even more opaque than before. Lili drifted deeper and deeper into the fog, moving away.

She heard the faint echo of a voice, her own voice.

– Lili! Lili!

Amalia woke up and tried to feel the sheet, the things around her, to orient herself. She reached for a glass of water on the bedside table, which fell noisily, shattering. She looked in surprise at the shards on the floor. So were her memories. Pieces of her life that she'd pieced together in vain, they couldn't make the whole complete. She was still under the influence of her last dream. She wondered if she really had dreamt it. After all, she thought to herself, is life nothing but a dream that arose in the eternity of sleep?

The next morning, they drank their coffee, discussing the weather, the pandemic, the changes in the country, and then set off for the cemetery, stopping on the way at a florist's.

– Take a bunch from outside and put the money on the stairs, the florist shouts.

– Do you have any other flowers inside? These look a bit prickly, asked Malvina.

– You can't come in. You're not wearing a mask. The woman was in a panic.

They stopped at a drugstore to buy masks and disinfectants.

– I'll give them to you, but they're no use, this virus passes through them.

– Well, then, why are we told to wear them? The pharmacist shrugs, clueless.

At the cemetery, they lit candles and arranged the flowers.

"If you saw us, what would you say, Mom?" Amalia wondered. She looked at Malvina. Usually, her face reflected her feelings, but this time it seemed blank. "Is she sorry? Is she apologizing to the one who loved her so much?" Amalia wondered.

After leaving the cemetery, they said no more words, as if the silence of the grave had enveloped them, speaking for them.

Once back in the apartment, Amalia takes refuge in the kitchen, preferring to cook, and Malvina is reading the novel she had just started.

— Have you ever wondered if I was happy with Dorian? Malvina tackled the subject over lunch.

The words sounded metallic and echoing, crashing against the walls, against the furniture, and then falling with a loud bang.

Amalia felt a sharp pain in her stomach. "My ulcer is bothering me again," she concludes. She tries to look impassive. "Why would you ask me that question, after all? What, have you wondered if I'm unhappy?" She did not voice her thoughts aloud.

— No, she answered instead.

— Such sorrow after all these years! Was it worth it?

— You've built your happiness on my unhappiness. And my mother's. Was it worth it for you? Amalia replied sharply.

— Amalia, it's been so many years...

— Time doesn't cure everything! Amalia drew her attention. Nor does confession absolve you of sin...

— No, but at least it brings the comfort of forgiveness, Malvina sighed.

— I'm not God, Malvina.

— Then, in the country, in Vultureni, I seduced Dorian. At first, it was fun. It amused me to see him watching me from the window as I showered in the garden, naked. Then, after that dance, we both snuck away from the house and he kissed me. I wanted to see Dorian kiss, and then, I thought nothing of it...

— I didn't know that since then... you...

Amalia closed her eyes out of reflex, or perhaps to hide her expression. She took a deep breath.

Most of the time, the trick worked and helped her regain her fluency of thought and speech.

— But somehow I felt it, Amalia confessed. After that visit to his parents, it was as if there was a ghost hovering between us, and we were no longer what we had been.

— I want you to know I didn't do it on purpose. I fell madly in love. And so did he. We both knew that by doing what we had done, we had to go far away, away from everything and everyone, if we really wanted to be happy... I thought so.

— And? Did you go? To come back to the question - was it worth it?

— Here, it was as if unseen threads were pulling me down, sinking me, and preventing me from springing... To answer your question - I'm not entirely clear. However, when I think that we were happy for a few great years, I think it was worth it. Too bad it didn't last. And I have a wonderful daughter, Marlene, and Dorian has been an admirable father. And for that, he deserved it!

"Does she realize how much she hurts me when she says that? Or does she do it on purpose?" Amalia wondered.

— I lived and loved intensely. Of all the men I've had, Dorian was the peak. And that was beautiful, although we had enough hardships. Strangers in a new country... Anyone, no matter what they say, starting a new life somewhere new isn't easy. Well, streets aren't paved with gold there... But we had each other. We made it through.

"Even now, you don't show a single sign of regret! You were only interested in yourself. You only loved yourselves! You tell me that isn't paved with gold, but you deceived my Lili with the American dream, where anything is possible! You've twisted her mind to rob me of the only joy of my life! Damn you, Malvina!"

Amalia's soul was boiling.

— Marlene's appearance in our lives had somehow affected our marriage. Strange, isn't it? I didn't want children, but Dorian wanted a lot.

"Don't mention it!" Amalia commented to herself.

— Marlene came back to him after the divorce...

"A child is not an object!" Amalia pointed out.

"Did you know I was pregnant when you fled the country? Did Dorian tell you?" It was a question Amalia hadn't asked herself since she had forced herself to stop thinking about the two of them. It was coming back to her now. She stubbornly avoided looking into Malvina's eyes.

— 'I didn't know you were pregnant when I left the country,' Malvina clarified as if reading her thoughts.

'And if you had, you wouldn't have gone with him? I can hardly believe you wouldn't. Would you have cared? You always got what you wanted without caring about anyone else!"

— Because of the baby, I lost my job, Malvina goes on. I just stayed at home. I felt like I was climbing the walls, going crazy with boredom. The only fun was going to the Orthodox Church once a month. Can you imagine? Me and the church! I was in pain and I couldn't bear to see our love dying! And then, by chance, I met Alex at a dance organized by a school on our street to raise funds for children with Down syndrome. You know, around there, if you want to be seen, you go to these charity events. Alex had been co-opted, being the main sponsor and having a granddaughter at that school. Very wealthy. He noticed me and that gave me confidence. We started dating... I was finally starting to come to my senses, to get my energy back, to live! I led a life of luxury with him. But don't think I didn't love him. I loved him. He was... how shall I say... brilliant. I left everything behind and started over... In case you ask me again if it was worth it... I guess it was. Fate doesn't ask you twice... Life is short, Amalia! Every moment it offers should be lived to the fullest. That's why I left his house with only one suitcase! My heels got hot for Johnny Prudel, so I closed one door and opened the next. Johnny was younger than me. I was afraid he'd find someone his own age... In fact, I was always afraid I'd be the one who got dumped! I was obsessed! Yes, Johnny was the first man to leave me. The poor, he had the bad inspiration to have a heart attack and the nerve to die!

Malvina twirled her fork several times in the noodle, watching, slightly absent, as the cheese spread. A couple of times, she opened her mouth to speak again, but closed it again. She wanted to say something meaningful, but felt unable to.

– Mmm! Cheese! I haven't eaten it in so long! I've missed the taste. A very inspired choice for lunch. I'll cook tomorrow. I'll buy some salmon. I'll pan-sear it with butter and sage. Do you like salmon?

– Not really... Amalia wrinkled her nose.

They hadn't broached such personal conversations since. They avoided them both, putting them off. Only a couple of times Malvina had asked her about her parents, and once she had tried to tell her about Marlene.

– Marlene is so different from me! she confessed to Amalia. She was very disappointed in her marriage... I told her that life doesn't end here, that there are still men in this world, but she pretended not to hear me... Recently, a co-worker of hers, Ed, would have wanted a serious relationship and she seemed to like him too, but I think she was afraid, and still is, to get too involved... You see.

She didn't go on, realizing that Amalia wasn't listening to her, doing her work in the kitchen, but also that she maintained a reserved and cold atmosphere, not telling much about herself. She concluded that she didn't want to share anything personal. She had been more introverted. Or maybe she didn't want to relive a painful past?

"Well, little by little, she'll come out of it. I just need a little patience," Malvina encouraged herself.

However, their time together did not bring the two women closer but, on the contrary, further emphasized the differences in their personalities, habits, concerns and deepened the already existing abyss. They were like two strangers living in the same apartment, and the state of emergency and the imposition of restrictions, with the isolation at home, exacerbated their inability to communicate their anxieties instead of bringing them closer together. They lost their freedom to go outside the walls of their home and a release valve, and their feelings remained trapped, unable to escape. Memories were taking clear shape; they wandered between them, silent and painful. Only the fear of the virus seemed to be common, to become a favourite topic of conversation, covering the depths of each of their souls like a thin layer of ice.

"With the power of thought, we conquer them all," Malvina encouraged herself. Sometimes, she gave voice to this thought, irritating her sister even more.

In the morning, they had coffee together. They talked a little and usually about neutral things, the weather, fashion, the latest news on TV. Malvina had opinions, and Amalia preferred to listen without debating, whether she agreed or disagreed - a self-imposed passivity. The only more animated moments were when Agatha came over, always unannounced. In Agatha's presence, things seemed more natural, conversations had substance. The woman also brought a touch of humour to the monotony.

For the rest, Amalia stoically endured her little sister's visit. Unfortunately, the pandemic was gaining strength, bringing unhappiness, isolation, sickness and the fear of death into everyone's lives. It was a war with unseen bullets, a war foreshadowing another war, like hatred that cannot be erased by forgiveness, like hatred that begets even greater, more intense hatred.

The tension between them risked shattering into words and became increasingly unbearable for both sides.

– I thought about renting an apartment, but with this pandemic and the isolation they're imposing on us, I don't stand a chance now.

– How long do you want to rent? Amalia asked.

– What, for how long? Forever, I told you! Malvina laughed so much that Amalia couldn't tell if she was serious. After all, Malvina had come with a suitcase and a hand luggage! To put in them the savings of a lifetime?

– Malvina continued in the same playful, ironic tone. Wouldn't you like to share our loneliness in our old age?

Amalia's eyes rounded in astonishment. It seemed to her that the proposal was quite indecent! How dared she mock her even now? She was speechless.

Chapter 18

— Have you gathered up Malvina's things? Have you decided when we're having her funeral? Agatha phoned her.

— Mostly, yes.

— And less, no? she joked. Come on, sweetie, the caseload's dropping. They said they could organize meetings if there's no more than 50 people. After all, it's not like a fair to have so many people!

— I'm thinking of postponing, maybe I'll get in touch with Marlene. Do you realize she hasn't returned my calls or messages? I mean, not even when I told her that her mother died.

— That's weird. Maybe they had a fight and we don't know... Maybe that's why Malvina decided to come back...

— I don't think so. I know Malvina talked to her on the phone after she came here.

— She must be like her mother! Not coming to Mom's funeral... Is that so?

— She doesn't look like she's reading the messages... I don't know, Agatha, I don't know where to find her. I went through Mom's things, maybe I could find her address, write her. I found nothing, really.

— I believe you. Nasty stuff. Anyway, let me know when you find her or when you decide. Listen, I've had a sore throat for a few days and I went to the family doctor to get checked out, but he's also hospitalised with COVID! The nurse wanted to test me. Uh, hey. Get out of here; I told her, this virus doesn't exist! She said she'd check for other viruses. Who was she trying to screw with? To fool me! I wouldn't let her. Well, other viruses you can easily knock out with a little traditional plum sanitizer. Come on, I got work to do.

— All the best, Agatha. Take care, Amalia advised her.

She had packed her clothes. She took the trolley from the shelf in the closet to put her sister's things there. She wanted to get rid of everything that belonged to Malvina.

In the outside pocket, she found a small photo album. There were several pictures of Marlene at various ages, the last one showing her mature, elegant, with her hair dyed a light shade. Amalia had never seen Marlene. The resemblance to Lili was striking.

In some of the pictures Marlene was accompanied by her parents. All cheerful, like in a publicity stunt, Amalia noticed. In one, they seemed to be somewhere on a beach. Palm trees here and there suggested an exotic place. An improbably beautiful sunset flamed all around. She also discovered a postcard of Alcatraz prison, with "San Francisco, Alcatraz" at the top and "I wish you are here" at the bottom. On the back, she found her name and a few lapidary lines: "Dear Amalia, I broke up with Dorian. I am only sorry for Marlene, our little girl, but I know she will be all right. Life goes on. I thought you might want to know..." As she read, Amalia's face changed. She hated Malvina, but she didn't suspect that Malvina hated her. At least, that was the conclusion she had drawn. Although postmarked, the postcard had never been mailed.

She took another photograph and shuddered. Lili! Lili at eight! Where did Malvina get this picture of Lili? Then she looked closer. The landscape was not native. On one side, there were skyscrapers, and the girl was a bit chubbier than Lili had been. They looked so alike.

In another picture were Malvina and Dorian beaming with happiness in front of a typical American cottage. How could they, knowing how much unhappiness, how much suffering they were leaving behind?

Then Amalia felt like she was suffocating. There was a picture of Lili arriving on American soil, accompanied by Marlene, and between them stood a thin, aged man. She barely recognized

Dorian; how age changes you! Amalia reasoned. And illness, too! she continued.

She remembered Malvina's equally suffering face from that day... She had also become distorted...

Chapter 19

Malvina was exhausted after struggling to breathe, and trying to get out of bed and go to the toilet resulted in her losing her balance and falling. Amalia helped her up.

— I've never felt so sick. I can't stand on my feet! Malvina stammered.

— All of a sudden?

— It started after breakfast. About an hour, I felt like throwing up, but I don't know why. All I had was toast with a little butter and tea. That tea you prepared for me. I took a metoclopramide, I thought I'd get over it, but I'm worse! I feel like I'm floating.

— I'm calling an ambulance! announces Amalia.

— No way! I'm afraid they'll put me in COVID area.

You've heard the horror stories... They put them in wards and they don't even go to see them... Amalia, do you think I have COVID?

— I don't know. How could you? We've kept out of it as long as we could. We haven't seen anyone lately! We haven't left the house. Well, until the grocery store. But you saw how many precautions we took!

— Yes, yes... Ouch! Malvina winces in pain.

— What does it hurt?

— Mm... Ow! My tummy! And I feel like I have no air!

— More tea. It's good for everything!

— I don't know...

He brought her a glass of tea, but Malvina found it made her nausea worse.

— I'll toast you another slice of bread. You may have an ulcer. I get them if I eat toast.

— I can't even swallow. I've never felt so sick in my life!

Amalia helps her wash. When she looked in the mirror,

Malvina was horrified.

— Is it me, or is one pupil bigger than the other? Ha! Ha! Ha!

— Why are you laughing? Nothing to laugh about. You really do have a bigger pupil! Amalia looked worried.

— "They are pale virgin's eyes, / As if enlarged by sorrows, / Casting shadows on minds, / From their comforting light." Remember when we used to recite it?

— Gosh, yes. I was in high school; I discovered some poems by Cincinat Pavelescu... How do you remember?

Amalia was amazed. She herself had forgotten this poem by Cincinat Pavelescu, which she had once liked! But that's how Malvina had always been, surprising! She had never let herself be overwhelmed, turning a smile on despair, going somehow against the grain. She had gone through life enjoying every moment, rejoicing for whatever reason, neglecting her troubles or simply avoiding them. Now, she was going right through them.

There was a strange pallor on her face, with darker patches emerging here and there.

— My God, how I loooook! This is how I imagined death! Help me get to my bed!

Malvina was again tense with pain. Amalia helped her, carrying her more on her back. She took her sister's hand in her palm, caressing it gently. Her pulse was getting weaker...

— How good you are to me, Amalia. I don't deserve it.
After all, I've done to you...

— It's been too much. What does it matter?
We're grown women now...

— Old, you mean, Malvina smiled.

— Just me.

— I made you suffer... and my mother too... Amalia lowered her gaze.

— Mother loved you. Mothers love their children unconditionally.

– They do...

Silence fell between them; disturbed every now and then by Malvina's laboured breathing and another bout of abdominal pain. She began to vomit, and the liquid was bitter and greenish.

– 'Tell me, Malvina,' Amalia broke the silence, 'why, after all these years, have you come back? You didn't come here for my sake, and I don't think homesickness hit you so suddenly. Your pension is nice, you've done well... Oh, and don't tell me you've come to join our solitudes, I don't believe you! So... What are you up to?

Malvina closed her eyes... She should confess to her sister... What? She had to say something to Amalia. Important! Very important! But what? Malvina became confused and exhausted, as if her life was running out. It seemed she could see her leaving.

– Where are you going? Malvina whispered to her illusion.

– I'm here, beside you, Amalia replied, surprised.

– I'm not asking you, she said with difficulty. Life. I'm asking it...

– I'm done. I'm calling an ambulance! Amalia started toward the phone.

– Forgive me... she squeezed Amalia's hand.

Amalia knew what it was like to be so exhausted that you can't speak, you can't move, you don't want to live. "No, no, Malvina! Only God forgives. I am not God."

– I have come... to help me... Aghh... Help! Help! she said in an increasingly muffled tone.

– Come in, Malvina, with the power of thought....

Malvina could no longer recognize the irony in her sister's voice.

Amalia shook Malvina vigorously, but Malvina had already turned blue and lost consciousness. Her hands were getting colder and her pulse was barely perceptible.

– Hello? Emergency? My sister is very sick, she has COVID, I'm sure of it. I did a quick test and it came back positive. She's barely breathing. How soon can you get here? Yes, definitely. Malvina Prudel, an American citizen, lives with me.

I'm her sister. Please come as soon as possible!

Yes... My name is Aludean Amalia. Yes... I'll give you the address... Urgent, please! Pleeeease!

Amalia shuddered as she remembered those moments. "I've come to help me!" a voice out of nowhere. And another answered, "I was behind the wheel."

– Shut up you all! Amalia waved her hands in an attempt to stop them, while at the same time; she was trying to dodge them.

It seemed to Amalia that she was one of the Goddesses of Hell, one of the Furies, perhaps Atropos. Definitely Atropos! she thought to herself. All sorts of crazy visions came to her, in which goddesses with beautiful faces and oily bodies gradually turned into monsters with discoloured faces, full of greenish blisters, dancing around a great fire, snakes slithering through the curls of their hair, growing larger and larger and more grotesque. From time to time, those faces grinned and then, suddenly, they took on the faces of Malvine, Cornelia and herself. It was the strange world in which Amalia was languishing, living it as if by herself.

Strange images haunted her another time, after her separation from Dorian, they disappeared after the birth of Lili, only to reappear with the arrival of Malvina. But since she had died, they'd gotten worse and scarier.

She took a few deep breaths. The voices stopped as suddenly as they had appeared. The images, too.

She didn't know what Malvina wanted to tell her. But who knows what's in the mind of a dying woman? Amalia wondered. Maybe the dying doesn't go forward to that final destination, maybe it rewinds life back to moment 0...

The ringing of the doorbell roused her from her meditation. She went to answer the door. It was Mrs. Grosu, the neighbour, with a large portion of croissants in her arms. Amalia was glad to see her, because it cleared away the gloom that had crept into her thoughts.

— Did you hear the upstairs neighbour is home? she informed him. And I hear her husband's back, too.

— Good heavens! I'm glad she's back. There's more good news in the world.

— Yeah, those cute little babies didn't deserve to be without a mom! But I'm glad to see, in their case, misfortune brought them back together. Not in the case of the Buru the family from the 5th floor. He was very angry and grumpy, unhappy about having to work from home. I heard she found messages on his cell phone chatting with his mistress, a co-worker. He packed his luggage and sent it to his mistress with a one-way ticket, not a return!

Amalia let Malvina tell her story without following it.

Chapter 20

She was back in Prosecutor Dinu's office. The same gloomy face, the same drab setting. The past weeks had not changed the atmosphere here, as if time had stood still. Only Dinu's unwillingness was new. It was clear to Amalia that after the harsh way, he looked at her, he no longer considered her a kind and nice 'granny.'

– You summoned me..., Amalia made an attempt to get his attention. She strained her voice.

– Mrs. Aludean, I called you here to give your consent so that we can have your sister disinterred... Would you object to that?

– No, I wouldn't... replied Amalia. I'd be delighted! She was put naked in a black plastic bag... like a dog. At least then, she could have a truly Christian burial...

– Perfect!

– Except...

– Except what? Dinu invites her to carry on.

– She had a daughter, Marlene. Shouldn't she give her consent?

– Hmm, yes, yes, I see... you also told me that she had a daughter when we last met, Dinu observes while leafing through the file.

– Yes. Perhaps I did. I don't quite remember... With age, you start to forget things...

– Meanwhile, you haven't been able to find her?

– Well, that's the problem, she's not answering her phone, she's not answering her texts... I don't know how to reach her. I've tried.

– I've started trying to contact the daughter, but it might take a long time and it complicates things..., the prosecutor pointed out.

That complicates things a lot... The prosecutor became

thoughtful, trying to find a solution. Hmm... You could make a statement that you tried to get in touch with the deceased's daughter but failed, so you assume to make all the necessary arrangements with the prosecutor's office, being the closest relative of Malvina Prudel in the country... Do you agree?

— 'Yes, of course,' replied the old lady with less conviction.

Amalia noticed that Dinu had brought out a printed declaration that she only had to sign.

— Why is the exhumation necessary? Amalia wondered.

— The hospital's morph pathologist admitted that the tissues didn't look like COVID infection, but like poisoning or something similar, but that, since the diagnosis on admission was COVID, he should have declared the death as well, that those were the recommendations, the protocol...

— Lord, protect and keep! How so? From what? With what? Amalia's astonishment seemed genuine.

— Are you sure you did a quick nasal swab and it came back positive for COVID?

— Absolutely. I told that to the doctor and the nurse who came home!

— Yeah, this COVID is full of surprises of all sorts, really. Anyway, we'll keep you informed! Dinu dismissed her, nodding briefly and getting down to work, immersing himself in reading another huge file - it must have had a thousand pages, on the cover of which Amalia had written: "The theft of two hens and a rooster from Vasilică Tărâță's garden."

Amalia did not miss the prosecutor's less relaxed tone. She got up from her chair. Her knees were soft. She wondered how they still held her. And her heart seemed to be still. She could no longer feel its ticking, but instead, she sensed the whiff of an undefined danger, which seemed to be becoming greater than the risk of contamination with the new coronavirus.

To Dinu's indignation, on the recommendation of the hierarchical chief, the file was closed for lack of evidence, not because anyone was looking for it, but because it was much more convenient, once Malvina Prudel had been declared "COVID-19 death" and had been buried in such conditions, for things to remain that way. It did not look good "digging up the dead," especially now, when the number of voices doubting the very existence of the virus was growing.

Marlene

My relationship with my mom had many ups and downs. I fondly remember my childhood, when there was more fun in our house, we went on vacations, and I was the centre of attention of my parents, happy to have me and I was happy to discover the world with them, a fairy-tale world in which I believed. Their divorce affected me and I was devastated when she insisted that I stay with my father and my paternal grandparents, a wish that I equated with abandonment, despite the fact that I adored my father. In many ways, this perception has remained similar over time. I often wondered what I had done wrong.

I had always considered her selfish, independent and shallow, but in terms of love, I loved her and I have the conviction that she loved me in her own way. It was hard for anyone not to hate Malvina! It was hard for anyone not to like her! My mother was always smiling; she had a contagious optimism that you couldn't possibly dismiss, even if you had a lot to reproach her for. Charming, I'd say now. She was like a bird, always willing to fly in search of freedom.

When the doctor told him he had leukaemia, after a moment of thinking, she smiled:

–Doctor, do what you have to do. I'll take care of the rest.

She emerged victorious, undergoing gruelling oncology treatments. Then she decided to travel the world.

When I was a child or a young lady, I didn't find much to praise her. The gifts she gave me seemed to tell me that she cared for me, that she hadn't forgotten me, even though she moved to another city with another man, even though we rarely spoke. She probably thought it was to compensate for her absence.

Still, she was there for me in the happiest, but mostly in the saddest moments of my life. When I, too, got divorced, I suffered because then it was not just a marriage that was falling apart, but a love – how sad it is to see a love passing away! Your dreams and hopes die. I closed in on myself, directed all my energy towards professional fulfilment, aiming to go higher and higher in the hierarchy of the company I worked for, to earn more and more money and appreciation and maybe, with a bit of luck, to be co-opted onto the Board of Directors. Instead, I had no time to develop a serious relationship, at least, that was the argument I came up with, convinced that "you can't have it all in this life", as my father often said. I found it hard to admit that I had become full of distrust, overwhelmed by the fear of being disappointed again, so I refused to get involved in a serious relationship. Lately, Ed has been trying to break down these emotional barriers, but afraid that he would succeed, I refused his proposal and asked him to leave me alone to remain just friends. But the loneliness I felt without him hurt.

"Life has some notable joys and many, many losses. It was another of my father's sayings, who, as the years went by, had become closer and closer to philosophy, without this saving him from the chronic depression he had been suffering from for some time. I was grateful to Lili that her arrival had changed my father's mood. At first, I didn't know the reason, convinced that my cousin's special nature, calmness, innate kindness and wisdom had as much influence on him as they had on me. We both looked forward to his visits.

She learned the truth about her birth from my father, and so did I. My father told her, apologizing for being late. We were both shocked, as when you discover a truth beneath a cloud of lies and betrayals. We were sisters! We couldn't believe it! During that time, we supported each other. She came to her senses quicker. I especially hated my mother when I realized that she had learned the truth many, many years before. But I learned forgiveness from Lili.

– I don't think I could ever forgive them, I confessed.

– Yes, you can. You can. Understanding. Loving. And when you love, you will forgive, she replied.

– Lili, can you really forgive? I realized that, although I had suffered from my parents' separation, the real drama had been hers.

– There's no point in being trapped in a past you can't change. You'd only perpetuate suffering. You must free yourself. Why would you want to see in a forest only a poison bush when it is full of beautiful trees? Forgiveness brings healing and hope. I believe so.

– What I wish I could believe the same, feel the same!

She gripped my palm with her palm, squeezing it gently. Her gesture was meant to give me hope.

Lili stood by me when my father died. But not only her, my mother also!

Mom! Always surprising! She always looked up and said to herself, she said to me:

– "That's why we have a life, let's live it, the good life, as it is! It's too short to dwell.

But when Lili died in that stupid car accident, I saw my mother, for the first time in my life, crushed and speechless. So was I. Lili was a beam of light!

In the following years, my mom and I began to grow closer and visit more often. After all, she was all I had left!

Towards the beginning of this year, around February, she told me that she wanted to go home, i.e., to her native country, without specifying when. Anyway, she sounded a little distant, uncertain. I didn't expect her to leave so soon. I never understood how one says "home" to a place she left so many decades ago and had only visited once. But it was her nature to do as she pleased, to answer to no one. Instead, I've learned to stop judging her, to stop judging anyone, to accept the people I care about as they are. I was worried, though, because there was a terrible pandemic coming with a new virus that mankind had never faced before. Some kind of alien...

But I calmed down when she sent me a message telling me that she was staying with her sister in Lugoj.

"Take care. There's scary news around here about the virus that's haunting the world."

"Don't worry," she replied. "I'm fine, as you know me. I love you."

I liked her. And she repeated this "I love you" when she called me one day from Lugoj. I reproached her again for choosing a bad time to travel, considering the pandemic.

— I'm looking for a donor, my dear. A stem cell donor.

She was laughing. How could she laugh when she said that to me? I got annoyed with her, but also anxious.

— You can't be serious! I replied, my voice choked with fear.

— I am. You know you took the compatibility test when I was diagnosed... and we didn't match...

— Yeah, good thing you didn't need a transplant. But why would you go out in the world looking for a potential donor? I asked her with a dark hunch.

— My disease relapsed, ruined my last shred of hope. And I'm not wandering the world, I've returned home!

— How long have you known about this? Maybe it's a mistake...

My voice sounded unnatural, drowned by a cry I could hardly hold back.

— Since the last check-up, just after the New Year. After so long. Who would have thought?

What a silly disease, really! Dr. Eyre gave me high hopes,

he told me that just as the disease responded to treatment the first time, it might respond the same way now, because new medication has come out... But you never know.

I'd rather take precautions. I hope I don't have to. I hope I'm a match for my sister.

She laughed out loud again, which seemed unnatural in the context of our conversation.

– What do you see funny now?

– Me, my sister and compatibility! Ha! Ha! Ha! She keeps laughing. It seemed like a joke only she understood.

– Well, we'll chat on other occasions. I love you, Marlene! Never forget that!

Then, I never heard from her or anyone. I was in a coma for almost a month, intubated. I had a miraculous escape. COVID had hit me in its ugliest form.

The first person I saw when I regained consciousness was Ed. He was sitting in a chair next to my bed. He looked tired, worried, with big dark circles around his eyes, a sign that he was severely sleep-deprived, and he had a beard that had been black for days. We looked at each other. I could read in his eyes a look of hope, of understanding and something else: a feeling that, by its warmth, disturbed me. I closed my eyes. When I opened them again, he was still there! For the next few days while I was in the hospital and then after I finally got home, Ed was a blessing!

As soon as I could, I turned on my cell phone. A bunch of messages! One of them caught my attention, being sent from an unknown number. "In two weeks, we're having Malvina's memorial service." It was dated May 31, 2020. I was shocked. I thought it was a mistake that someone had found a morbid way to make jokes at my expense just now. Could his leukemia have been so advanced that...? I couldn't pronounce the word. It couldn't be true. I looked upstairs. There was another message sent earlier, April 20th, also from the same number:

"This is your aunt, Amalia Aludean. I bring you the painful news that Malvina, your mother, has died of COVID. There will be a funeral in three days at the Central Cemetery in Lugoj, because COVID deceased can't be kept any longer. I will give her a Christian burial. I hope you can come."

I took a deep, very deep look at those messages. Mom had died! That free, bird-like flight had been broken! That constant flight from herself had ended. I was out of breath for a moment. I felt as if a star had just fallen and drowned in the sea. Various feelings tormented me. I couldn't believe I was going to talk about my mother in the past tense.

I immediately phoned.

– Hello! Mrs. Amalia Aludean? I am Marlene...

I am Marlene.

– Marlene? God, girl, I texted you, I called you...

– I was in a coma, COVID... Mom? Mommy? How... Choked with tears, my question had become a whisper, unable to continue...

She told me that my mother had had COVID, a severe, rapidly progressive and fulminant course. I could barely stand. I was still dizzy and my heart was going crazy – the after-effects of the infection... Ed had offered to stay with me until I got better. I could tell he'd been waiting for me to tell him to stay for good, but even though I felt it as a necessity, even though I panicked every time he walked out the door and I was alone, my words were still delaying their presence. I was going to start treatment to recover, to get stronger. I wanted to go to Lugoj, to see my mother's grave, but in the condition I was in, it wasn't possible yet.

It wasn't until three months later that I got well enough to go.

I announced my intention by telephoning Aunt Amalia. On a beautiful September day I arrived in the small town in the province of Banat. I was watching all the details through the window of the rented car at the airport in Timisoara. Compared to New York, Lugojul, with its old and cozy buildings, its almost palpable tranquility, with the Mureș lazily flowing through the middle of the city, seemed to me to be from another world and another time. Lili grew up here... And my mother had also died here! I already felt connected to it, to that place.

It was relatively easy to find the address of the apartment where my aunt lived. I knocked briefly. I waited a while. Then, a very wrinkled, white-haired woman with a kind face opened the door. That was Amalia, my aunt, Lili's mom.

– Lili!

The woman's words seemed to come from somewhere far away, from another time. We didn't hug, we didn't shake hands, but the way she said the name had something special about it, like a kind of prayer, or rather a kind of "Thank you, Lord, You" that we say when our prayer has been answered.

- I'm Marlene, Malvina's daughter, I introduced myself, a little confused.

Amalia didn't say anything, as if she hadn't even heard me, just stroked my head in a way that broke my heart. She had a lost look.

– Lili, I've been waiting for you to come!

I didn't know what to say or how to react, but the happiness in her eyes stopped me from correcting her.

She took me by the hand and, rather awkwardly, I went inside, letting her lead me in. The woman seemed happy! She took my suitcase and put it in the hallway, then invited me to sit "where I fancy sitting." I got the impression that she was talking to me as if we'd known each other forever and as if we'd seen each other the day before. That surprised me because I was never at ease. She was going around, serving me coffee, biscuits. And rose marmalade she made especially for me, knowing I liked it!

I couldn't remember ever tasting anything like it. I reluctantly took a spoonful. Very good indeed!

- Don't fill up! I know you're hungry, but it won't be long before dinner time and I'll heat up the food too. I made your favorite! Eggplant salad, giblets soup and stuffed peppers!

I just wanted to ask her what giblets meant. I hate stuffed peppers. When I was a child, my grandmother, my father's mother, cooked them for me. It made me so sick that I could never eat peppers again, no matter in what form they were cooked.

I ate very little. She started to tell me about the neighbors in the block, about the fact that some old buildings in Lugoj were being renovated, assuming that I knew them, about a lady teacher who had recently died...

— The summers have gotten stifling here because of global warming. It's not like when you were a child, she told me.

I remember watching her stunned, instinctively feeling it better not to contradict her. After clearing the table, she took my suitcase from the hallway and led me into a room. I guessed that it had been Lili's room because on the desk by the window was her framed picture propped on a small tripod.

— See? I kept the room exactly as it was when you left. Nothing has changed, my darling.

Let me make the bed in case you're tired and want to lie down.

I tried to help her, too. I was amazed at the joy on her face. Then she pulled a little box in blue velvet out of a drawer and handed it to me. I opened it slowly with great curiosity. It was an old ring, blackened with age, but it had a beautiful amber, with many golden iridescences, a play of light and shadow.

— It's yours! she said. Put it on your finger.

— Mine? I wondered.

— Yes, yours. I should have given it to you before... Look! It suits you! she exulted after I put it on my finger. How nice it looks on your hand!

— Yes, it's a beautiful stone. Thank you. Thank you.

— Did you know it comes from the resin of ancient trees? If you look closely, you can even see little fossil inclusions from different ages... Aren't they full of mystery? Like the human soul. It also keeps the past within itself, with joys and sorrows... Especially pain. These pains, ah, they poison the souls! she nodded with regret. Come, I'll let you make yourself comfortable.

Left alone in the room, I sat down on the desk chair. I picked up Lili's photo as if the mere touch of her could bring her close to me. I stared at it for minutes.

Then I took a long look at the amber on my finger. I thought about what Aunt Amalia had said. Yes. The human soul also gathers a mixture of feelings of its own existence of those before it, which can remain captive, just like the ancient fossils in this stone.

"You can. Understanding. Loving." I winced. The words once spoken by Lili suddenly awakened from memories, relieving them.

I picked up my cell phone and dialed Ed's number. He answered immediately. I realized he had been waiting for my call. I confirmed to him that I had arrived safely, but also that I intended to stay longer than I had planned, wanting to get to know this old lady better, feeling that I owed Lili a debt. Ed couldn't hide his disappointment. I took a deep breath and, afraid not to back down, I uttered:

– Ed, I love you!

There was a deep silence at the other end of the line, which panicked me.

– Ed?

– I'm sorry, Ed. You took me by surprise. I was speechless! Do you have any idea how long I've been waiting to hear you say that? If I asked you to marry me now, would I have better luck than last time?

– Absolutely.

– Why don't I take a longer vacation and come stay with you in Lugoj? From there we could go and visit some places in Europe, if you want to, of course... That way, it'll be like a honeymoon, only we'll do it before we get married! I take the first flight, what do you say?

– Are you crazy? I asked him, laughing.

– I'm crazy about you! And I don't even want to give you the chance to change your mind!

All that first evening, I was in a good mood, listening to Aunt Amalia with great patience and forbearance.

– Tomorrow I'd like to go to my mom... er... Malvina's grave, I told her. Could we?

– Of course!

The next morning, after breakfast, Amalia took some sprigs full of green, fir-like leaves and some candles from the vase.

– We take them to the grave, she explained. Pity they don't have flowers this time of year! 'Taxus baccata,' she said, raising her eyebrows, looking as if she was sharing a great secret with me. Yew! It blooms in winter and spring!

– I don't think I heard.

– It's an interesting shrub, evergreen, and the flowers are red, in the shape of little candles, very beautiful... And very poisonous, she added after a pause. Never make an infusion of them...

The cemetery was a little further away, but we preferred to walk at an easy, strolling pace. The weather was nice, neither too hot nor too cold. Behind some fluffy clouds, the sun was hiding, coming out every now and then, caressing our faces with its golden rays. On the way to the cemetery I would notice the yew shrubs, evenly and elegantly cut, which so beautifully adorned this small but charming little town, and realize that I had seen them elsewhere, in other lands, many times.

Malvina Prudel was buried with her mother and father. They were all reunited after so many bitter years, and I found it touching.

Amalia arranged the yew branches neatly in two elegant stone holders on either side of the cross, lit several candles and then began to pray. I did the same. I looked at her face. She was serene and... lost.

When we finished our prayers, she took me by the arm, urging me to go away, I replaying memories that I didn't want to talk about for fear of bursting into tears, and Amalia walked beside me, immersed in silence and in her own thoughts.

– Where are we going?

– We're going to meet Agatha! she replied automatically. You haven't seen her for a long time.

In fact, I had never seen her and I didn't even know who she was!

She stopped in her place, looked at me with an unsuspected tenderness and stroked my hair as she had done when I had arrived.

Countless golden iridescences glittered in her eyes, like the amber of the ring that now adorned my hand.

– Never leave me alone, Lili, ever! Never leave again, my daughter... Don't ever go away...

About The Author

Simona Mihuțiu is a Romanian writer whose voice resonates across multiple literary genres. Born on July 13, 1966, she balances a distinguished career as a practicing medical oncologist with a prolific life in literature. Her ability to navigate both the clinical world and the creative realm gives her writing a unique depth and emotional authenticity.

Mihțțiu is the author of four novels, including her latest, Sick Bonds (Total Publishing, 2024), a compelling exploration of human connection and vulnerability. Her earlier works—Window to Tomorrow (2019), Destiny, a Spoiled Toy (2021), and It Could Be Me (2023)—established her reputation as a thoughtful storyteller with a gift for emotional insight.

Her contributions to short prose are equally notable. Works such as Free to (not) Think (2021), When Facts Find You (2023), and Stories from Mister Help (2023)—translated into Spanish as Cuentos de Señor Help—showcase her versatility and wit, ranging from memoir and humor to philosophical reflection.

A talented playwright, Mihuțiu has seen two of her plays published: Hope Never Takes the Elevator (2023), which continues to enjoy success on the stage of the Queen Maria Theatre in Oradea, and Temptations of Glory (2025). Her dramatic work has been translated into Spanish (La esperanza nunca sube en ascensor) and French (L'espoir ne prend jamais l'ascenseur), further extending her reach to international audiences.

Mihuțiu's poetic voice is both introspective and evocative. Her four volumes of poetry—Geometries of Soul (2021), Lost Seconds of Poetry (2022), Whispers from the Spiral of Silence (2024), and May It Still Make Sense (2024)—delve into the intricacies of time, silence, and the human experience.

Beyond fiction and poetry, she is also an essayist and literary critic.

Her essays in Beyond LIKE (2024) engage with modern culture and thought, while her critical work, Traveling Among Words. Stopovers (2024), reflects her deep engagement with the literary world.

With over 50 published articles and contributions to numerous anthologies and collective volumes, Simona Mihuțiu stands as a vibrant and essential voice in contemporary Romanian literature. Her work continues to inspire readers both at home and abroad.

Contents

www.ingramcontent.com/pod-product-compliance
Lightning Source LLC
Chambersburg PA
CBHW071426300726
48976CB00004B/1259